W9-BAC-734

PRAISE FOR THE FILM

Woman, Thou Art Loosed!

"Ferocious . . . startling . . . a more sobering and credible
experience than most other modern 'inspirational' films . . .
leaving little doubt that [T. D. Jakes] is a man capable of
changing lives and leading a flock."

—*Variety*

AND BISHOP T. D. JAKES

"To me, there is no man of God who is more gifted,
more compassionate, more articulate, more anointed to
reach and touch lives, small and great, than T. D. Jakes."

—Oral Roberts

"Bishop T. D. Jakes is a breath of fresh air."

—Natalie Cole

Also by T. D. Jakes

HE-MOTIONS

FOLLOW THE STAR

GOD'S LEADING LADY

THE GREAT INVESTMENT

MAXIMIZE THE MOMENT

THE LADY, HER LOVER, AND HER LORD

HIS LADY: SACRED PROMISES FOR GOD'S WOMAN

T.D. JAKES

WOMAN, THOU ART LOOSED!

BERKLEY BOOKS, NEW YORK

THE BERKLEY PUBLISHING GROUP
Published by the Penguin Group
Penguin Group (USA) Inc.
375 Hudson Street, New York, New York 10014, USA
Penguin Group (Canada), 10 Alcorn Avenue, Toronto, Ontario M4V 3B2, Canada
(a division of Pearson Penguin Canada Inc.)
Penguin Books Ltd., 80 Strand, London WC2R 0RL, England
Penguin Group Ireland, 25 St. Stephen's Green, Dublin 2, Ireland (a division of Penguin Books Ltd.)
Penguin Group (Australia), 250 Camberwell Road, Camberwell, Victoria 3124, Australia
(a division of Pearson Australia Group Pty. Ltd.)
Penguin Books India Pvt. Ltd., 11 Community Centre, Panchsheel Park, New Delhi—110 017, India
Penguin Group (NZ), Cnr. Airborne and Rosedale Roads, Albany, Auckland 1310, New Zealand
(a division of Pearson New Zealand Ltd.)
Penguin Books (South Africa) (Pty.) Ltd., 24 Sturdee Avenue, Rosebank, Johannesburg 2196, South Africa

Penguin Books Ltd., Registered Offices: 80 Strand, London WC2R 0RL, England

This book is an original publication of The Berkley Publishing Group.

This is a work of fiction. Names, characters, places, and incidents either are products of the author's imagination or are used fictitiously, and any resemblance to actual persons, living or dead, business establishments, events, or locales is entirely coincidental.

Copyright © 2004 by T. D. Jakes.

All rights reserved.
No part of this book may be reproduced, scanned, or distributed in any printed or electronic form without permission. Please do not participate in or encourage piracy of copyrighted materials in violation of the author's rights. Purchase only authorized editions.
BERKLEY is a registered trademark of Penguin Group (USA) Inc.
The "B" design is a trademark belonging to Penguin Group (USA) Inc.

ISBN:0-73499-4707-6

PRINTED IN THE UNITED STATES OF AMERICA

WOMAN,
THOU
ART LOOSED!

PROLOGUE

1984

Giggles erupted, carried on the wind in the backyard of the house on Lockhart Avenue.

Sunlight danced among the tops of the trees, scattering shadows across the grass as a little girl crouched down behind a tall oak tree that held a broken swing and asked, "You ready?"

His eyes tightly shut, the little boy trembled in anticipation. "I'm ready."

"Open your eyes."

He did as he was told.

She jumped from behind the tree, put her hands to her mouth and shouted, "Ladies and gentlemen . . . presenting . . ." She paused a heartbeat before spreading her hands in a dramatic fashion. "Meeeee!"

Captivated, his eyes never left her face. She looked so pretty—just like an angel to him.

Rising up slowly, she began to sing. "Little Sally Walker, sitting in her saucer . . ."

Gyrating her hips, she moved from side to side. "Rise, Sally, rise . . . Wipe your weeping eyes . . . Put your hands on your hips and let your backbone slip . . . Awww, shake it to the east . . . awww, shake it to the west . . . awww, shake it to the very one that you love the best . . ."

She shook her hips toward the little boy, who couldn't seem to stop staring at her with his mouth hanging open. Although she couldn't explain it, she knew somehow she'd performed magic.

1

20 years later

The cathedral was filled to capacity.

Thousands of people from all walks of life filled the pews on the bottom and in the balcony on the last night of revival. It was a hot June evening, and the warm air combined with the body heat from the congregation made the church service a little uncomfortable.

She didn't care though. She was on a mission. She knew something was going to happen. She could feel it. Her stomach quivered from the anticipation of what was to come.

Tonight her life would change.

She made her way slowly through the sea of people, her arms clutching the purse as if it were her very lifeline.

She was ready for the pain to end. She was ready to give this thing that had a choke hold on her life over to God.

For the first time in a long time, a spark of possibility burgeoned within her breast—there was a chance to change the person she had become. She could be made whole again. . . .

It seemed to take her forever to make it down to the altar. There were so many people ahead of her, filling the aisles. Like her, they wanted to unburden their souls—be washed clean of their sins and begin life anew.

She stole a glance over her shoulder and saw that there were even more people behind her, forming a line. She wiped at her tears with the back of her hand with no care of the damage done to her makeup. She wanted forgiveness. She needed it.

She yearned for peace of mind. She wanted to feel safe and secure. She needed to just be able to *feel* again.

She had listened attentively—she'd heard the encouraging words Bishop Jakes spoke. They filled her with something that had eluded her for most of her life. *Hope.*

She drew closer, amidst the crowded sanctuary, to the altar. She was ready to place her wounded soul before the Lord. Here she would pour out her pain and rage over all the things that went wrong in her life. Here she would beg for His forgiveness and vow to serve Him.

It was here that she would find acceptance and redemption.

Her heart leapt with joy when she made it to the front of the massive church. She opened her purse and reached inside to pull out a painful reminder of the past—tangible evidence left over from the day her childhood and dreams had died.

Scanning the different faces gathered at the altar, her eyes landed on one person in particular. Shock filled her to the core, followed by disbelief and finally white-hot rage mingled with stark fear.

The gun suddenly appeared from out of nowhere and three shots were fired, sending people screaming and running all around the sanctuary.

In the midst of growing panic and fear, the woman collapsed to the floor.

2

"Black man walking . . . ," a female voice called out over the steady clicking of the heels from a pair of shoes making their way down the long corridor.

Klip klop . . . klip klop . . . klip klop . . .

"Is that him?" an inmate asked. "You know, that preacher on TV? Bishop T. C. Jakes?"

"T. D. Jakes, stupid," another one corrected.

Klip klop . . . klip klop . . . klip klop . . .

The sound of his shoes echoed throughout the hall and maintained a steady pace.

Bishop Jakes could hear muffled whispers coming from behind the cold steel bars that separated the cells. He ignored the suggestive remarks a few of the inmates made and continued to walk forward with authority and purpose.

"Hey, we don't get much company on death row. How about sendin' a sista with a smile on her face?"

Although he looked straight ahead, from the corner of his eye he could see inmates standing with their faces and warm bodies pressed against the bars. Some held out small mirrors, hoping to catch a glimpse of him. For some, he was the only celebrity they would ever see.

Another inmate grumbled, "I ain't impressed. He ain't nuthin' but a man. . . ." The voice belonged to a woman wearing a buzz cut. "Just like me." She cackled at her own wittiness.

A ring of laughter rang out around Bishop Jakes but he continued to ignore the whistles and catcalls.

"What they charge you with, preacher man?"

His heart quickened at the words of the inmate who pleaded, "Can you pray for me, Bishop? Please tell Jesus about me. . . ."

Another inmate hollered, "Yeah, pray for me too. . . . Pray that I get my hands around the throat of the snitch that dropped a dime on me."

All around him whoops of laughter bounced off the walls.

The footsteps of the guard slowed and stopped in front of a cell at the far end of the corridor.

Bishop Jakes followed suit. He had reached his destination.

The jangle of keys against the metal locks reverberated throughout the corridor, but the girl sitting cross-legged on the floor in that last cell didn't bother to look up. She continued to focus her attention on whatever she was working on.

From where he stood, Bishop Jakes couldn't tell what it was or what it was supposed to be.

Although in her early twenties, she could pass for much younger, despite the hardships she'd been forced to endure.

"You have a visitor," the guard announced. He held the cell door open and stepped aside to allow Bishop Jakes to enter.

Upon closer inspection, Bishop Jakes found that the young woman was gluing a matchstick onto the skeleton frame of a small house.

The room was bathed in a long uncomfortable silence.

"Hello, Michelle," Bishop Jakes greeted her after a moment.

No response. Her eyes remained fixed on her task as she picked up another matchstick and applied it to the house.

"May I sit down?"

Michelle Jordan continued to work on her project, pointedly ignoring him.

"The warden told me about your hunger strike."

Silence.

Just when he thought this visit had been in vain, Michelle chuckled under her breath. "Now that's funny. I started a fast."

The corners of his mouth turned upward. "I guess that is kind of funny."

There was another long silence, and Bishop Jakes raised his eyes heavenward.

"The key to building a strong house is the foundation," Michelle began. Her hand trembled as she continued to glue matchsticks together. "Most people think that the biggest threat comes from what's outside. The elements. But you gotta be real careful what you put inside."

Not sure what to make of her comment, Bishop Jakes took a

seat in the only chair in the room and inquired, "How are they treating you?"

Michelle didn't respond to his question. Instead, she replied, "One time I finished building my house but forgot that I left a tube of glue inside. When the sun got hot enough it just caught fire and imploded from the inside. Once that happens, it's just as good as gone. Be careful what you leave on the inside."

Giving him a sidelong glance, she asked, "Can you get up for a second?"

"Excuse me?"

"If you're planning on sneezing, that's the wrong end." Michelle managed a small, tentative smile and pointed to the chair. "Can you pass those tissues?"

Realizing he'd sat down on a box of Kleenex, Bishop Jakes stood up. He picked up the smashed box and held it out to her.

Michelle pulled out a tissue and wiped off the excess glue from the matchsticks in her hand.

Bishop Jakes decided to come straight to the point of his visit. "You wanted to see me?"

"I didn't think you'd really come," she admitted with a nonchalant shrug. "I saw you on the cover of *Time* magazine. 'Is this man the next Billy Graham?' Now you don't really expect somebody like you to take a stroll down death row to preach to the likes of me."

"I'm not here to preach to you," Bishop Jakes stated. "I'm here to reach out to you."

Her eyes, sharp and assessing, traveled over his face briefly. "They say a man's grasp should always exceed his reach."

"You've been on my mind ever since it all happened," Bishop

Jakes confessed. "I keep wondering if there was something that I could've done to help. You were so close. And then . . . I can't help but feel responsible."

"So you here to clear your conscience?" Michelle gave a slight shrug. "No need, Bishop. All you do is come here, give us false hope and leave. I'd heard about prison ministries but I never really understood the point. I mean, what kind of an offering can you take up? Cigarettes, some weed maybe? . . . Besides, none of us are gettin' out of here. We're the lifers, the hopeless cases. Ain't no rehabilitation going on. No souls you can save here. . . ."

As she talked, Michelle's mind traveled back to the events that led her to death row.

Michelle scrubbed her body until her skin tingled. She wanted to wash off all the remnants of prison life—the anguish, the oppression and the guilt. She longed to be far away from this place, from all it represented, from all she had become.

The spray of hot water trickling down her body sent Michelle's thoughts back to a scene in the past—one that stayed along the dark edges of her mind.

In the memory, she saw a little girl—she became the little girl—sitting in a tub with the shower running, scrubbing her body raw, trying to wash the feeling of filth from her skin. Michelle shook her head, trying to dislodge the image from her brain.

"Nooo," she muttered, when the memory became too real.

Michelle ignored the curious glances she was receiving from a group of inmates standing a short distance away. She knew they wondered what was going on with her, but Michelle wasn't interested in sharing. She didn't tell anyone she was leaving. Haters never want you to leave them behind.

On her way out of the prison bathhouse, Michelle tossed one of the women her bar of soap. She wouldn't be needing it anymore. Drug possession charges and her attack on her mother's boyfriend had landed her in prison, but she had done her time, paid her debt. She was getting out of here. Michelle intended to make the most of her freedom—she wasn't about to travel back down this road again.

Prison life. She didn't want nothing to do with it.

Michelle stood before a woman wearing a guard's uniform and holding a clipboard of official-looking documents.

"You must maintain strict adherence to the rules of your parole. Any violations thereof will be cause for further incarceration. There will be no affiliations with known felons, no drug or alcohol use, and no possession of firearms. You may not leave the state under any circumstances whatsoever without the express written consent of your parole officer. You will be subject to random drug and spot testing as determined by your parole officer. . . ."

Michelle retained her composure as another guard bent down to apply a LoJack on her ankle, tangible proof of her probation and house-arrest status.

She accepted the large paper bag from another guard, held out to her without a word.

The guard picked up a package and said, "This is for you, too."

Michelle held the paper bag in one arm and a care package in the other. She knew exactly what was in the bag. A purse, a blonde wig, a tube of bright lipstick, stiletto-heeled shoes and a dress that had hugged her body like a glove—all the things she had on and in her possession when she was arrested. The only thing missing was the drugs that had been in her purse at the time.

Stopping at the first garbage can along her path, Michelle poured the contents of the paper bag in the trash. She didn't want any reminders from her past life. But then she reached back in and pulled out the purse. She could still make use of it.

Michelle tore open the care package; inside was a blue-and-white sweatsuit.

She smiled as she read the note.

Thank you, Twana, she whispered. Her godmother never failed to send her whatever she needed or put money on the books for her.

Her head held high, Michelle tucked her new clothes under her arm and began her final walk down the corridor, trudging forward to freedom.

"Twana, I need you to pick up Michelle from the bus station tonight. She getting out today. I . . . well, you know it's Reggie's bowling night . . . I'll talk to you later. . . ." Cassey kept her message short and hung up the telephone. She really didn't know what else to say.

"You ain't have to tell her all that. I don't want that big-mouthed Twana in my business. She always got somethin' to say and I'm tired of it."

"Reggie, don't start with me," Cassey warned. "I ain't in the mood for no fightin'. I had to tell Twana somethin' since I'm asking her to do me a favor. I don't know why you won't just let me keep the car so I can pick up my own daughter. You can catch a ride with one of them no-good friends of yo's."

"I'm takin' the car, Cassey. I bought it—"

She cut him off by asking, "What you say?" Cassey shook her head. "Ooh nooo. I bought that car out there with my hard-earned money. You ain't worked a j-o-b since I met you. You sho' don't bring no money in here."

Reggie advanced toward her. "I'm real tired of you throwing that in my face."

Cassey didn't bat an eye. "I ain't throwing nothin' in your face but the truth."

In a surprise move, Reggie wrapped his arms around her. "You better be glad I'm crazy 'bout you, woman."

She struggled to keep her resolve and pulled away from him. "Get off me, Reggie. I'm mad at you."

"Can't you see it?" Reggie questioned. "Cassey, that girl ain't even out of prison good and she already got us at each other's throats. Now this house been peaceful-like since she been gone. The minute she on her way back—we fightin'."

"Michelle is my child, Reggie. I can't just ignore her."

"I ain't asking you to. I'm just saying you need to remember how much trouble she caused when she was livin' here." Reggie shook his head. "I don't trust her. I can't sleep in this house as long as Michelle is here, Cassey. I ain't trying to tell you what to do—just telling you what I feel."

Cassey released a long sigh. "I'll figure somethin' out," she muttered as she walked into the kitchen.

Reggie let out a quiet curse.

They were letting Michelle out of prison after only three years? What was this world coming to? He shook his head in disbelief.

He ran his fingers along the scar on his chest. It still bothered him every now and then.

A chill ran down Reggie's spine as he noted just how close Michelle had come to stabbing him in the heart. She was an ungrateful witch.

Reggie thought about all the gifts he'd given her when she was growing up. He thought of how he used to even help her with some of her homework until it became too challenging for him.

He acknowledged that he had not been a shining example of fatherhood, but Reggie believed he'd done the best he could.

"Michelle can't come back in this house," he whispered.

Reggie glanced around to see if Cassey was anywhere nearby. "No siree . . . she ain't coming back here. You can't stab and disrespect me like that. This my house."

He cursed. "I'd have to sleep with one eye open 'round here. . . ." Shaking his head, he added, "I ain't doin' that. Michelle bet' not bring her crazy behind to this house. I don't wanna have to hurt her."

3

Recalling that she wasn't alone, Michelle drew her attention back to the present. Her eyes were misty and wistful.

"What surprised me the most, Bishop," she stated, "was you getting the warden to approve my early parole. Now that's pull. You didn't know me from Adam. And I never attended any of your services. All because my mother asked you."

Her eyes had suddenly become flat and as unreadable as stone. "About the only thing she ever did for me."

She picked up another matchstick and continued, "Three years in lockup is a long time. I'd made up my mind that the person walking out of there would be a lot different than the one they dragged in. Problem was, I really didn't have anything to go home to. Don't get me wrong. It ain't like I didn't appreciate going home. But it came with strings attached."

Michelle's mouth turned downward. "Everything comes with a catch."

Bishop Jakes kept his voice calm, soothing and without judgment. "Your mother seemed to think that church revival was just the thing you needed to turn your life around. The warden seemed to think so, too. That's why he made it a stipulation of your release."

Michelle glued a matchstick to the door of the tiny house. "I guess even the warden didn't think I'd do something that crazy. Yep, three days at revival sure did change my life forever. . . ."

Dead silence.

After a moment, Bishop Jakes inquired, "Why don't you tell me what was your childhood like?"

"Black."

He wore a puzzled expression. "I'm afraid I don't understand."

"I called my grandmother *Mama* . . . my mother by her first name, and her boyfriends *Uncle* . . . does that answer your question?"

"Cut that singing out," Cassey demanded when she walked out of her bedroom. "And look at this place. . . . Girl, you got toys all over my new leather couch. . . ."

Michelle's eight-year-old body trembled at the sound of her mother's voice. Her homework momentarily forgotten, she immediately began to straighten up the living room to avoid her mother's wrath.

She stole a peek at her mother, who was dressed in a tight-fitting black dress that barely covered her breasts.

She sure is pretty, Michelle thought. When I grow up, I wanna look just like her . . . be just like my mama.

"Michelle, what you still doing here anyway?" Cassey fussed. "I thought I told you to go to Twana's house a while ago. She's babysitting you tonight."

"She wasn't home," Michelle replied. "I got scared when it started getting dark, so I just came back here."

"Well, I've got to find somebody to keep you. I've got a da—" Cassey stopped short, paused a moment, then began again. "I've got a meeting tonight."

"With who, Mama?"

"What did you call me?" Cassey asked as she confronted her daughter, her eyes narrowing.

"Cassey," Michelle corrected. Feeling intimidated, she backed away from her mother.

"There you go. I had you way too young." Cassey picked up a stuffed bear and tossed it to Michelle. "Your Uncle Reggie is gonna be here any minute."

Cassey plumped and straightened the bright red-and-white pillows that adorned the black couch. "I want this place to look nice."

She gestured with her hands. "Now pick up those toys. I don't want this place looking like a pigsty."

Setting the bear on top of the glass coffee table, Michelle searched her memory. "I don't know any Uncle Reggie. Is he my new uncle?"

"Just do like I told you and quit asking me a bunch of questions," Cassey snapped impatiently while she went around the room straightening the pictures on the wall and wiping down the

shelves on the entertainment center with her hand. "Good-
ness . . ."

Michelle was still focused on the idea of having a new uncle. "I got lots of uncles, but how come I don't see them more
than once?" she questioned, giving her mother a sidelong
glance.

"That's because you so messy and hardheaded. Yo' grandma
gonna have to keep you 'cause I can't take this. You wearin' on my
nerves, Michelle."

Hurt, Michelle took an armload of her toys to her room and
dumped them into her toy box.

A few minutes later, she returned to the living room to get the
rest. This time Michelle decided to remain silent. Cassey always
seemed to be in a bad mood whenever one of her uncles was
coming to visit. She wished Twana had been home.

Michelle loved her godmother because Twana was nice to her.
They could talk about anything. She and Cassey barely talked
about anything—her mother was always too tired, too sick or
getting ready for a meeting. But Twana always made time for her.

Cassey reached for the phone and dialed. "I don't know why
Twana did this to me," she muttered under her breath. "Wait 'til I
see her. . . ."

Checking her watch, she stated, "Yo' grandmama better be
home."

"She said to call her Mama-Mary because she's too young to
be a grandmother."

Cassey rolled her eyes. "Please . . . Granny better act her
age. . . . Hello, Mama. . . ."

While she talked, Cassey ran her fingers through her hair in a nearby mirror. She stood there admiring herself while she talked. "You wanna see your granddaughter tonight?

"Mama?" Cassey stared at the phone. "I like her nerve. . . ." To Michelle she announced, "I think your grandmother hung up on me."

Dropping her head, Michelle hid her smile.

Cassey had just put down the phone when it rang again. "Hello, Mama?"

Michelle watched the range of emotions that washed over her mother's face.

"Twana, where you at?"

Cassey groaned. "I can't wait 'til your nails dry. Reggie's gonna be here soon." Shaking her head in frustration, she said, "I don't care if you got to take them off and stick 'em in the oven."

The sound of the doorbell ringing sounded through the house.

"Shoot! He's here. Hurry up, Twana." Hanging up the phone, she turned to Michelle and asked, "How do I look?" Releasing a short laugh, she muttered, "Why am I asking you? You don't know how to come in out of the rain."

Michelle's eyes grew wide and her bottom lip trembled slightly, but Cassey paid no mind.

The doorbell rang out again and again.

Cassey straightened her dress and rushed to open the front door.

Michelle stole a peek from where she was standing. The man was tall and slender. He held out a bouquet of flowers and flashed Cassey a devastating smile before asking, "You want my arm to fall off?"

"Oooh, Billy Dee said that in *Lady Sings the Blues*." Cassey giggled.

So this is Uncle Reggie, Michelle thought as she studied his dark chocolate-tinted face. He seemed nice enough. Her eyes traveled back to her mother. Everything about Cassey fascinated her. Michelle adored her.

Cassey took the flowers from Reggie and held them to her nose, inhaling deeply. "These are beautiful, Reggie. Thank you. Please come in," Cassey purred, batting her eyelashes.

Michelle batted her own eyes, mimicking her mother.

Reggie stepped inside the house and Michelle moved to the sofa, sitting down with her arms folded across her chest, observing Cassey and Reggie in silence. Her mother had completely forgotten all about her and the fact that she hadn't finished cleaning up the living room. She seemed to only have eyes for Uncle Reggie. It was always like that whenever one of her uncles showed up. That's why Michelle didn't really care whether they ever came around again.

"Life is so ironic," Michelle heard Cassey say. "One day we're standing behind one another at the unemployment office, and the next day, you standing right here in my house."

Reggie gave a low guttural laugh. "That's what happens when you slip your number in my pocket."

Cassey gave him a seductive smile. "I believe in going after what I want."

Their eyes locked hungrily.

"And I believe in giving a woman just what she wants," Reggie responded after a moment.

Michelle quietly noted the way Cassey held her head when

she laughed and the way she flirted with Uncle Reggie. Michelle couldn't help but wonder if she would see him again after this night. She'd never seen Cassey act like this before.

Her eyes met her mother's gaze.

"Reggie, this is my daughter, Michelle."

He turned to her as if noticing her for the first time and gave Michelle a big smile.

"Nice to meet you," she mumbled.

"Michelle, go get my mauve purse," Cassey ordered. "I'ma take it tonight."

"I don't know where it is."

Her mother glared at her. "Then find it."

"Find it where?"

"Get in there and look for it," Cassey demanded. "Or I'll find it in your butt."

Michelle stomped all the way to the bedroom. She could still hear them talking as she searched through her mother's closet for the purse.

". . . That girl's a handful ever since her father died . . . she's this close from me sending her to live with her grandmother."

"That's what you get for having her so young. What were you? Thirteen?"

Cassey grinned. "Aren't you sweet? Can I offer you something to drink?"

"No, thank you. I don't want to spoil my appetite. We're going to Antoine's for dinner."

Michelle couldn't find the purse Cassey was talking about, so she positioned herself near the door and listened to the conversation between her mother and Uncle Reggie.

"That's a really nice restaurant. Ain't cheap, either. You sure know how to impress a woman. Keep this up and you might get what you want."

"Only thing is, my unemployment check won't start for another week or so. You don't mind fronting me until then, do you?"

"Oh . . . uh . . . not at all. I can pay for dinner. A week, you say?"

"Or so," he mumbled.

"Sure, I can handle that. Her father left her a small trust that she draws from every month. Check just came today. I'll just get my purse."

"Keep this up and you might get what you're after tonight."

"Michelle, hurry up with that purse," Cassey yelled.

"I'm looking," she responded. "But I don't see it."

"If I come in there and find it, I'ma use it to go upside your head. Now get out here and keep Uncle Reggie company while I get it. . . ."

Michelle sauntered back into the living room, wondering why her mother had practically chased her into the bedroom in the first place.

"Would you excuse me? She can't do nothing right." Cassey gave her a frustrated look. "Michelle, get him something to drink while I look for this purse."

"Yes ma'am," she murmured, wanting to please Cassey. Anything to keep her from yelling at her.

Her mother disappeared down the hall while Michelle made her way to the kitchen.

Humming softly, Michelle poured Uncle Reggie a glass of water.

"How old are you, Michelle?"

She jumped at the sound of his deep voice. She hadn't realized Uncle Reggie had followed her to the kitchen.

"Eight," she responded.

"Eight, huh? You're kinda big for an eight-year-old. Kids these
days develop faster than girls did when I was growing up. I think
it's the steroids they putting in the food these days."

The way he was staring at her made Michelle uneasy.

He took a step toward her, asking in a low voice, "You know
what it means to develop?"

"No sir."

"That means you gonna start filling out like a grown woman.
In two or three years you'll be stacked up right."

His eyes continued to rove up and down her body.

Michelle had no idea of what Uncle Reggie was talking about
or why he was looking at her that way, but deep down she knew
it didn't feel right.

Suddenly wary, she held out the glass to him, backing away
when he reached for it.

"Ain't nothing to be scared of," he tried to assure her. "When
the time is right, you'll welcome it."

His eyes traveled down her body again, his gaze pinning
her to the wall. Unexplainable fear snaked down her spine.
"Mommy . . ."

The doorbell sounded, breaking Reggie's probing gaze.

"Get the door, Michelle," Cassey called out.

Brushing past Reggie, she ran all the way to the front door.
Throwing it open, she was relieved to find Twana standing there.

"Hey, Michelle, you ready to go? Don't forget your pajamas.

Your mama gonna pay to get my nails done if—" She stopped short. "You all right, baby?"

She didn't know what to say. Michelle couldn't put words to what she was feeling. Uncle Reggie made her feel funny—no, that wasn't it. He scared her.

Twana's eyes traveled past Michelle.

"And who are you?" she asked.

Reggie sipped on the ice water, his eyes never leaving Michelle's face. After a moment, a smile spread across his thin lips as he responded, "Uncle Reggie."

Reggie's eyes boldly appraised Twana from head to toe.

She stiffened, noting his dark and insolent eyes. Dogs averted their eyes when caught, but not this man—he was a snake. A predator.

She sent a warning glare his way before glancing down at Michelle. "You okay, honey?"

"Uh-huh." Michelle clung to Twana as if her life depended on it. "I'm ready to go. . . ."

Twana looked up at Reggie again then back down at the girl. "But you're okay, right?"

A frown set into Reggie's features.

"Whacha trying to say?" he asked.

Unafraid, Twana opened her mouth to respond but Cassey burst into the room, saying, "I found it."

Surprise registered on her face. "Twana, when did you get here?"

"Not too long ago. Not a moment too soon, I'd say. . . ." Her eyes traveled back to Reggie.

He gave her a cocky smile.

Sensing the tension in the air, Cassey eyed Reggie and Twana warily. "What's going on?"

"Ain't nothin' going on, baby," Reggie answered thickly.

"Michelle and I are leaving," Twana announced after a moment. Playing with the barrette on the little girl's head, she added, "Ain't we, sweetie?"

"Come give me a kiss," Cassey ordered.

Michelle did as she was told. She prayed her mother wouldn't ask her to give Uncle Reggie one, too.

"Good-bye, Michelle," he said smoothly, with no expression on his face.

Michelle waved.

Twana took her by the hand and led her to the front door, saying, "Come on, sweetie. Let's go. Let me get you outta here."

"If you were my daughter . . . ," Twana muttered under her breath.

"You say something?" Michelle inquired.

She shook her head no. "Go on and get in the car."

Twana strolled around the car to the other side and climbed inside. She turned to Michelle. "Honey, you sure you okay? You'd tell me if something was wrong?"

The little girl nodded.

"Now I want you to listen to me. Stay away from Reggie. Ya hear me, Michelle?"

"Yes ma'am."

"I need to have a lil' talk with your mama," Twana uttered as she pulled away from the curb. "I don't like the looks of that one."

4

Bishop Jakes could hear the voices of the other inmates calling out to one another, their conversations splintered. He watched the painstaking effort with which Michelle worked on the framing of the tiny house.

"Your mother took that day off so that she could pick you up. The day you got out of prison. I wonder why she didn't."

Michelle cut her eyes at him. "C'mon, Bishop. Stevie Wonder could see that. The devil wouldn't let her." Her voice was heavy with sarcasm.

"Michelle, people give the devil far too much credit."

"No," she countered. "I think people underestimate him. He ain't just that fire-breathing guy with the pitchfork. The devil lives in that run-down one-story house on Lockhart Avenue. It looks small and harmless now, but it felt like a prison back then."

She paused for a moment before adding, "That's an exaggeration. Prison was never quite that bad."

Bishop Jakes looked at her, his eyes urging her to go on, but Michelle changed the subject.

"You know, it's funny. No matter how far you go, how much time has gone by, you can never really escape your past. I thought getting out of prison would be a fresh start for me. You know, start clean. Hmph, guess there ain't no soap strong enough to wash away my mess. Nah, the past has a nasty way of sticking to ya."

She'd been waiting on Cassey to pick her up for the last two hours.

It wasn't quite night, but inside the bus station Michelle could feel darkness descend upon her as she observed loved ones picking up relatives.

Another hour passed, then another.

Four hours later, the station was empty except for Michelle and a cleaning lady.

Michelle took one last look at the clock before walking out of the train station and to the nearest bus stop.

She boarded a local bus ten minutes later.

The ride wasn't that long, and before she knew it Michelle was stepping off the bus and walking the one and a half blocks to her childhood home on Lockhart Avenue.

When she was a little girl, her home seemed so huge, but now—now it looked like a tiny bungalow compared to some of the newer homes nearby. It used to be white with black shutters, but in the three years she'd been gone it had been repainted a pale yellow with blue trim. Michelle didn't have to wonder who picked those colors. *Reggie.*

Her stomach began cramping as she stood across the street, beneath a huge oak tree, staring at the place that now held so many unpleasant memories for her. The three-bedroom house that was supposed to be a refuge instead had become the place she was running from.

"Welcome home."

She started at the baritone voice coming from behind her.

Her defenses up, she whirled around, demanding answers. "How do you know me?"

"Little Sally Walker, right?"

Michelle eyed the tall, handsome man. "What you call me? . . ." She'd seen those warm brown eyes before . . . that funny smile. . . . She took a step forward for a closer look.

Recognition dawned. *"Todd? Is that you?"*

Grinning, he nodded. "The one and only. I came back to stay with my mother."

Michelle folded her arms and gave him a sidelong glance. "I heard you got married and everything."

"Yep. And I have a little girl . . . four years old."

"You married. . . . Who? . . ." Michelle paused for a moment before continuing. "Uhh . . . don't tell me. . . . You married Keisha Taylor?"

"Word gets around."

She couldn't resist saying, "You know in school, people used to say she looked like me?"

He laughed. "Yeah, I know."

Michelle couldn't get over how handsome he'd become. She

hadn't seen Todd in ages, but he was still able to set her pulse racing.

Todd's eyes traveled the length of Michelle's body then back to her face. "It's real good to see you."

"You look good. . . ." She eyed the faded blue jumpsuit he was wearing. "For a janitor."

Todd gave a small laugh. "I had some plumbing problems. Every now and then I like to get my hands dirty."

"Mission accomplished."

He pointed to the house across the street. "So, how long you home?"

"*Home?*" Michelle shook her head and folded her arms across her chest. "That ain't my home. It's just a place where a piece of me is buried. I won't be staying in that house."

"So where you living then?"

Michelle handed him a piece of paper. "That's the halfway house. There's a bed there with my name on it."

"My bed used to have your name on it."

A little surprised by Todd's forthrightness, a slight smile emerged on Michelle's face. "Well, all I need right now is a lift. How 'bout that? Can you help out an ol' friend?"

"At your service. . . ." He pointed to a Ford Explorer. "My car is right there."

Michelle followed Todd to the automobile. He held the door open for her.

"Still a perfect gentleman, I see," she murmured as she climbed inside.

As Todd drove, Michelle listened to the radio, singing softly.

"I love to hear you sing. You have a nice voice."

Michelle burst into laughter. "Yeah, right, Todd. Just keep driving."

When Todd pulled into the driveway of the halfway house, she uttered, "Thanks for the lift."

Michelle reached for the door handle, but his voice stopped her.

"Do you have to go in right this minute?"

She sat in the car contemplating for a moment while Todd played with the radio. He was probably searching for some mood music, Michelle decided.

"A special engagement only at the cathedral, the one, the only, Bishop T. D. Jakes. . . ."

Michelle placed her hand on his to keep him from changing the channel when she heard Bishop Jakes saying, "Remember, where you are does not define where you are going. This will deliver you from frustration. God has a plan for your life. Keep your eyes on the prize. When Peter did this, he was able to walk in what other people sank in."

Another voice chimed, "Get there early. Friday, Saturday and Sunday. At the cathedral located on . . ."

Leaning forward, Michelle turned off the radio.

"Why you so interested?" Todd asked. "You going?"

Rolling her eyes, Michelle nodded and said, "Yeah. As a stipulation of my parole . . ."

"Huh?"

Michelle threw open the car door. "Look, I gotta go. Thanks again for the lift, Todd."

"My pleasure. Will I see you again?"

Gathering her things, Michelle shrugged. "Maybe tomorrow night. At the revival . . ."

She climbed out of the car and strolled up rickety steps to an old three-story house. Without having to look across her shoulder, Michelle knew that Todd was still parked in the driveway.

Waiting for what? she wondered.

She knocked on the front door.

Behind her, Michelle heard Todd start the car and pull out of the driveway. She refused to look back because she didn't want to give him the satisfaction. Instead, Michelle continued staring straight ahead.

She heard a lock turn and the door opened a crack. "Yeah?" a woman's voice questioned.

Michelle could only glimpse a partial view of her face. "I'm supposed to be staying here."

"Can't let you in after curfew," she stated in a clipped voice.

"Look, my bus just got in and nobody was there to pick me up," she huffed. "I'm Michelle Jordan."

The door slid open wider.

"Michelle? Girl, you don't know nobody? It's me. Nicole."

"Nikki?"

"Yeah. It's me."

Removing the chain from the door, Nicole whispered, "Come on in before Delores wakes up. She's the nosy witch in charge here."

She opened the door wider and peered over her shoulder. "C'mon. Hurry up."

Stunned over running into her childhood friend, Michelle tried to move but her feet wouldn't budge—it was almost as if they were glued to the wooden porch.

"Hurry up. . . ." Nicole pulled her inside and closed the door behind her.

Inside the foyer, Nicole questioned, "Girl, what are you doing here?"

"I should be asking you that," Michelle shot back. "This is the last place I figured I'd see you. I don't believe this. You got a husband and two kids."

Shaking her head, Nicole responded, "Not anymore. He took them the last time I went into rehab. I hear they moved to Atlanta. It's not that far away, so I hope he'll bring them to see me soon."

Michelle gave her a sympathetic look. "That's too bad. I'm sorry."

"Don't be. I wasn't no good to any of them. I just need some time to get myself together."

"You will," Michelle encouraged. "Just one day at a time, right?"

"It's hard though," Nicole confessed. "I had to borrow money from Pervis just to send my kids something for their birthday."

Michelle's eyebrows rose in surprise. "Pervis from the strip club?"

"Who else? Don't you still owe him money?"

Shrugging in nonchalance, Michelle replied, "Yeah, so what? Tell him to bill me. He lets his girls smoke for free until they get hooked. Then you gotta strip to pay a pipe debt. Ain't that how you lost your family?"

"No," Nicole answered. "I lost my family because I like to smoke crack."

"Either way, there's a bullet with his name on it."

"Girl, keep that kind of talk down if you don't want it to get back to Ms. Rodgers."

"From the parole board?"

Nicole nodded. "She don't play that. She show up here anytime she want to, usually unannounced, trying to catch somebody doing something."

"Well, all she'll catch me doin' is sleeping at revival."

"Revival?"

Michelle burst into laughter. Shaking her head, she said, "*Revival. Can you believe that?*" In a louder voice, she added, "So all you gonna find here is *complete compliance.* You hear that, Miss Rodgers?"

"Shhh. . . ." Shaking her head, Nicole muttered, "You still crazy."

"That's why I'm going to revival. You know what, Nikki? You oughta come with me."

Nicole laughed. "I don't think so."

Leading the way up the stairs, she stated, "I'll show you where you gonna be sleeping. We're sharing a room."

She and Nicole grew up living next door to each other. Now here they were, sharing a room in the halfway house. Michelle thought back to when they were little, playing with their dolls and planning their dream weddings.

Michelle dreamed of becoming a famous singer. Nicole dreamed of becoming a model or a fashion designer. The closest Nicole ever got to fulfilling her dreams was shoplifting in fine department stores, while Michelle's dreams were squashed by the time she was twelve.

She and Nicole were close—almost like sisters. They'd shared many secrets over the years, experimented with drugs together and stripped together at the club.

"Look at us," Nicole stated. "Back together again."

"Yeah," Michelle agreed. "At least this time we get to keep our clothes on. I know more about you than I care to know."

"Hey, I can say the same thing 'bout you."

Nicole handed Michelle a pillow. "I borrowed it."

Michelle sniffed it.

"Don't worry, it's clean. I washed it earlier today when I found out I was getting a roommate."

"Nikki, how long you been here?"

"Not long."

Michelle sank down on the bed assigned to her. "So, how is your mom? She still livin' over there on Lockhart?"

Her smile disappearing, Nicole shook her head no. "She died last year. She had cancer."

"Nikki, I'm sorry. I didn't know."

"I was so messed up, I didn't know nothin' 'bout it until a month later."

"We traveled some rough roads," Michelle acknowledged. "But this time we're on that street called Straight."

Nicole agreed. "I wanna be with my kids. I can't be messing up no more."

"I ain't going back to prison," Michelle vowed. "That life ain't the one I want for me."

Michelle looked at her friend and smiled. Man, life sure did a number on them. A recovering junkie and an ex-con.

But it was nice to see a familiar face. For the first time in a long time, Michelle didn't feel so alone.

When the clock struck midnight, Michelle and Nicole were still talking.

"Remember when we used to have those old perverts slobbering when we stripped . . . ," Nicole was saying. "Girl, there were some sickos in that place."

"What else you expect to find in a strip club?" Michelle

switched positions as she tried to make herself comfortable in the twin bed. "Normal people don't pay to see a bunch of women dancing around naked."

While they talked, Michelle's mind traveled back to her days at the club. She could almost smell the stench of sweat combined with alcohol and smoke. She could still hear the patrons yelling out obscenities as they tossed damp dollar bills at her semi-clothed body gyrating onstage.

"Earth to Michelle . . ."

"Huh?"

"What you thinking about?" Nicole inquired. "You got quiet on me all of a sudden."

Michelle lay on her side and used her arm and hand to support her head. "I was thinking back to our days in the club. I remember Pervis, with his stupid self, over in that corner working his deals. He made a lot of money selling drugs at that table."

"He sho' did." Nicole shifted positions in her bed. "Know what I remember?"

"What?"

"Remember when old Charley Mason jumped on that guy over Lisha?"

Michelle fell back in the bed, busting up with laughter. "Charley got his tail whupped good that night. He in there fighting over Lisha and she didn't care nothing for him."

Nicole joined in the laughter. "He actually thought she was in love with him. I kinda felt bad for Charley."

"I didn't," Michelle stated as she sat up in bed. "I didn't feel sorry for none of those freaks in the club." Her mouth turned downward. "They made me sick to my stomach."

During those days, Michelle made sure she was good and high before getting up on that stage. When she was high, she didn't have to think about what she was doing—the drugs provided her a temporary reprieve from her life.

"How'd you get here tonight? Did your mom bring you?"

The air suddenly became filled with tension.

"Haven't seen my mama," Michelle responded after a moment. "Todd drove me over. Remember him?"

Nicole shot up in bed. "Really? *Todd Barker*?"

Michelle nodded.

"Girl, I ain't seen him in ages. Is he still cute?"

"He's all right." Michelle kept her voice nonchalant. "To tell the truth, he still look good, but right now I can't think about Todd in that way. Besides, the man is married. And I got to concentrate on fixing me."

"But y'all still friends, right?"

"Yeah, I guess so," Michelle murmured. She closed her eyes, summoning up an image of Todd and his sexy grin.

Michelle yearned for the stolen moments she and Todd shared a lifetime ago. She sighed softly.

He was married now—it was way too late for them.

Seeing her again sent Todd spiraling down memory lane.

When Michelle dropped out of high school and disappeared without a word, he was left feeling hurt and humiliated. After meeting and marrying Keisha, he'd allowed himself to believe that he was long over Michelle.

But just now, when she was sitting in the car with him, it felt like old times. He still felt like a teenage boy experiencing his first crush. Michelle's nearness still made his senses spin.

I guess it's true. You never really get over your first love.

The short span of time he'd spent with Michelle earlier forced him to acknowledge that his whole being had been filled with waiting—waiting for her return.

Todd couldn't deny that there was something different about Michelle. Gone was the light that used to dance in her eyes when she smiled. He was entranced by the silent sadness of her face.

Prison life changed her.

Todd wasn't sure this woman recently released from jail could ever be the Michelle he'd fallen in love with, but maybe . . . maybe in time she would. Or at least give him a clue where his Michelle had gone. The one who'd dreamed of becoming a star—a big-time singer. The one who was by no means blind to his attraction. They'd been good friends and lovers until the day she disappeared.

Nursing a broken heart, Todd attempted to move on with his life. He married Keisha.

A real bad mistake, he decided.

All his life, Todd had only one woman on the brain. Michelle Jordan. He yearned for the little girl that could always make him smile, her gaze holding him captive for hours on end. He wanted his Michelle back—the one filled with big dreams and aspirations.

Life had dealt Michelle a cruel blow, changing her into this broken woman who no longer had a smile—even for him.

Looking up toward the heavens, Todd whispered, "I want her back. I want my Michelle back."

5

"You've certainly been through a lot," Bishop Jakes said, looking at her with compassion.

Michelle went back to working on her house, pointedly ignoring his gaze. "I ain't proud of what I've done. It sure wasn't what I had planned. But I did what I had to do . . . or at least I thought so at the time."

"I'm not judging you, Michelle," Bishop Jakes said kindly. "I'm just saying it must have been difficult to go through that, to feel so—"

Michelle snapped her head up and cut him off. "Look, don't feel sorry for me. I don't want your pity. And dancing in the club wasn't so different from what I was used to. Men leering at me, looking at me in a sexual way, devouring my body with their eyes. . . . Shoot, men have been looking at me that way as long as I can remember . . . even in my own home."

Michelle chuckled and continued, "You know, at least the club legitimized it. Made it a business transaction. I knew a lot of girls who used their body just to get a little attention, find the love they weren't getting anywhere else. Love, right? Hah. What a joke. They wasn't getting anything but played. At least I was getting paid."

Michelle looked him right in the eyes and questioned, "Bishop, do you know what it's like to feel that all yo' worth is below your shoulders and above your knees? Well, I figured if I had it, I might as well use it. Yeah, I used it. What else did I have?"

She slowly shook her head back and forth. "You know, even with all that, I still thought I could change. Get back on my feet, make something of myself, get myself together. . . . Yeah, right. My Mama-Mary used to say, 'You can dress up a donkey with ribbons and bows, but in the end it's still just a sorry ol' ass.' People are what they are. Things don't change . . . no matter what we want to believe."

Twana held the phone up to her ear with her shoulder as she permed her client's hair. "Girl, let me tell you what he did after that. When he came home and saw his son in bed with the mailman . . . he like to—"

She stopped mid-sentence when Michelle and Nicole burst through the doors of her shop.

"Girl, I gotta go. My baby girl is home. You do way too much gossiping for me. . . . And you know what they say—a dog that brings a bone carries one right back with him."

Grinning, Twana hung up the phone and ran over to greet Michelle with a hug.

"Michelle? Girl, look at you. When I heard you were coming home I nearly danced outta my weave."

Michelle gestured toward her companion, asking, "You remember Nicole?"

Twana gave the young woman a hard, cold-eyed smile. "Hmmmmm . . . sho' do."

Picking up her purse, Twana handed it to a coworker. "Go hide this in the back."

When Michelle sent a sharp look her way, Twana shrugged in nonchalance.

"You talked to Cassey?" Michelle inquired. "I called the house all morning and she never answered."

"Well, you know that Reggie's on dialysis. She gotta take him up there to handle his business." Twana's face was marked with loathing. "If it was up to me his kidneys would be the size of cantaloupes."

"She didn't pick me up at the bus station last night."

"I know," Twana confessed. "It was Reggie's bowling night. She left me a message to come and get you. But I didn't check my messages yesterday until late. You know I woulda been there otherwise."

"Some things never change," Michelle muttered.

A flash of humor crossed Twana's face. "I shoulda sent that fine Todd to pick you up. Girl, you should see him now. He all muscular and so handsome."

"I have."

Twana frowned. "I certainly hope you weren't looking like that. You might've scared the poor boy away."

Shrugging, Michelle responded, "My mind ain't even on no man, Twana. I don't even remember what it feels like to be a woman."

Twana placed a hand to her chest. "Ooh noo. Girl, please don't tell me some big burly woman turned you out in there."

"Pleeze. . . ."

"Michelle, you're a beautiful girl," Twana complimented. "You just need to stop lookin' like you just finished shooting an *Oz* episode."

"Well, this is what I am now. Anyway, Todd says he might be coming to revival tonight."

"All he's gonna feel with you lookin' like that is sorry for you." Twana reached down and pulled a bag from under the sink. "Look at this . . . I bought you something. A welcome-home present."

She pulled a dress out of the bag, saying, "They said it was one size fits all. . . ." Twana held the dress against her ample body. "But I know that's a lie."

Michelle gave her a grateful smile. "You didn't have to do this, Twana. I mean, you sent me that care package." Pointing to the sweatsuit she was wearing, she added, "You even got my size right."

"I know I didn't have to do it—but I did. Now shut yo' mouth about it." To the people in the salon, Twana said in a loud voice, "Everybody, come here. Look who's home. Y'all come welcome Michelle back home."

Her coworkers and a few of the clients gathered around Michelle and Nicole.

Michelle was uncomfortable with all the attention focused on her. "Twana . . ."

"Michelle, you remember Pumpkin, don't you? She's gonna have your hair out of sight." Patting her own hair, Twana murmured, "She put my weave in. Everybody says it looks real."

Taking Michelle by the arm, Twana steered her toward a Korean woman sitting at a table. "This here is Pok Chu . . ."

The woman awarded Michelle a timid smile.

"Pok Chu . . . ," Twana began, "manicure, pedicure. . . ."

She whispered to Michelle, "She act like she don't speak no English, but watch tellin' your business around her." Then she smiled at the Asian woman and continued loudly, "She can put everything but a fine man on your nails . . . and don't forget them crusty toes, Pok Chu," Twana stated with a laugh.

She pointed to a slender man standing nearby. "That there is Delicious."

Michelle gave him a tiny smile.

Whispering, Twana said, "His mama named him Chuck. Go figure. Anyway, don't nobody do makeup like that child."

A man entered the shop selling hats, purses, shoes and accessories.

"Roscoe . . . wait right there. We need you."

Twana turned toward Michelle. "Make yourself comfortable 'cause you'll be here a while, girl. You 'bout ta get made up, under, around and over," she said and laughed.

· · ·

Twana observed Michelle.

She looked good . . . healthy, but sad. *Cassey should've picked up her daughter last night at the bus station. She can't keep putting Reggie's needs over Michelle's. She needs to remember she's that girl's mother.*

Unconsciously, Twana placed a hand to her belly. Over the years, she'd had plenty of chances to be a mother, but threw them all away.

The time just wasn't right . . . the man wasn't right . . . she wasn't right. . . . Each time she got pregnant, Twana headed off to the abortion clinic.

Now years later, she was left with nothing but regret and guilt.

Michelle was the closest she'd ever get to having her own child and Twana determined to be there for her—no matter what.

She felt somewhat responsible for the way Michelle turned out. She knew deep down that Reggie was doing something to her, but Twana couldn't get through to Cassey. She'd even tried to convince her to let Michelle live with her.

Cassey wouldn't hear of it.

Twana and Cassey even went through a period of not talking to each other for a few months when Michelle was twelve.

She and Cassey were best friends. They'd been through a lot together, were always there for each other. As little girls, Twana would wrap her arms protectively around Cassey and let her cry herself to sleep those nights that she stayed at Twana's house, es-caping the unspeakable horrors that went on in her own home. Later, Cassey did the same, comforting her friend after each abortion and truly believing her when she said she would never let this happen to her again. And when it did, Cassey never once threw it up in Twana's face.

Yeah, they always had each other's backs, but when this thing with Reggie and Michelle started, Twana just couldn't stand for it. That girl needed someone to protect her.

I feel like I failed you.

Twana's eyes filled with tears. She wiped them away and walked over to where Michelle was seated.

"I'll see you later at the church. Okay?"

Michelle nodded.

Twana blew her a kiss and strode to the back of the salon. She came out a few minutes later with her purse.

"I'll see y'all tomorrow," she said on her way out the door. "I can't be late for the revival."

In her bedroom, Michelle spun around slowly in her new dress. It fit her slender form perfectly. Twana had chosen wisely.

She didn't like frilly dresses, preferring a more simple design instead. The long summer dress with the soft pastel floral print made her feel feminine. Her godmother had even purchased a pair of lavender mules, a perfect match to the dress for Michelle to wear.

"Girl, you look beautiful," Nicole murmured. "That dress fits you real nice. Twana got good taste in clothes."

Standing with her hand on her hips, Michelle wanted to know, "Can you see the LoJack?" She didn't relish wearing the label of ex-convict, but had no choice for the time being.

Nicole shook her head. "Not really. You have to really be lookin' for it."

Feeling self-conscious, Michelle checked out her reflection in the mirror. She pulled on her dress and asked, "You sure I look okay?"

"You look fine, Michelle," Nicole reassured her. "Now stop tripping and go to the revival." She laughed. "I can't believe you going to church. Girl, things sure have changed."

"Yeah," she muttered. "Hopefully for the better." Michelle played with her hair, fluffing up the spiral curls.

Tossing a look over her shoulder, she said, "Nikki, I think this is way too much makeup. They'll be able to see my face long before I even step inside the church."

"Girl, you crazy. Your face is fine. Will you go on and leave? You look great."

She wondered what Cassey would say when she saw her. Michelle grabbed her purse. "Okay. I'm out. See you later."

"Hey, I'll wait up for you. In case you running late."

"Okay. Thanks."

"Tell Todd I said hello."

"If I see him."

"Oh, you'll see him. Todd was crazy in love with you. He used to hang around us all the time begging for some attention from you."

"The man has a wife," Michelle reminded her friend.

"And?"

"This coming from a woman with a husband." Michelle shook her head. "You really need to come to revival with me."

Nicole laughed.

Outside her room, Michelle took a deep breath and walked down the stairs.

Cassey primped and preened in the mirror, making sure every hair was in place before leaving the bathroom.

"Woman, I got to go," Reggie shouted through the closed bedroom door. "If you want me to drop you off at that football-stadium-sized church, then you need to hurry up. I'm leaving in a few minutes . . . whether you ready or not."

Cassey shook her head in disgust. "I bought that car," she muttered. "He better not leave me. . . ."

She stepped up the pace and grabbed the pink-and-white purse that matched her suit.

"Cassey," Reggie yelled. "C'mon now, woman."

"I'm coming," she yelled in response. "Just wait a minute. . . ."

Cassey stormed out of her bedroom. "I don't know why you in so much of a hurry. It ain't like you got to be anywhere important."

Reggie waved off her comment. "Just bring yo' slow behind on before I change my mind. I ain't in the mood for yo' crap tonight."

"You can change yo' mind all you want, Reggie—I can drive myself."

"Drive what?" Reggie inquired with a short bark of laughter. "You ain't taking my car nowhere."

Cassey stuck her chin out as she folded her arms across her chest. "Yo' name ain't nowhere on that car out there. Don't go tryin' to get on yo' high horse with me."

Anger flashed in Reggie's eyes. "Take yo' car then. I don't want that old piece of a Cadillac anyway. I can get plenty women in the street to buy me a car. Put it in my name, too."

Challenging him, Cassey pointed to the door. "Go on then . . . probably what you been doing all along . . . messing with other women."

Reggie eyed her for a moment. "If I wanted to be with them, Cassey, I'd leave. I'm here in this house 'cause I want to be."

"You sure that's the reason?"

"What other reason could it be, Cassey?"

Without responding, she walked out the front door. "I need to get to church, Reggie. I'm selling the tapes tonight and I need to make sure everything is set up. You was in such a big hurry a few minutes ago—well, let's go."

6

After a soulful rendition of "Blessed Assurance," the choir, draped in royal purple robes with gold trim, took their seats as Bishop T. D. Jakes stepped up to the microphone.

"Are we happy today?" he asked the audience.

Some members of the congregation yelled "Yes" in unison, while others shouted "Hallelujah."

"Let's go to the book of Genesis, verse thirty-seven line three," Bishop Jakes instructed. "We are all familiar with the story of Joseph. Tonight I want to use the subject, 'The Favor that Fathered a Child.' I used to think it was the other way: 'The Father that Favored a Child.' But it is our Father's favor that births all greatness."

Looking around, trying to absorb everything, Michelle was overwhelmed by the size of this mega-church. There were people milling about everywhere. She waded through the crowd of bumping elbows, bodies darting here and there, hoping to be able to find Twana or even Cassey. Her search appeared futile because there were thousands in attendance for the revival.

A young man came up to her and touched her elbow. "Can I help you?" he asked.

"Got room for one more?"

The deacon burst into a short laugh. "Praise God. Your first time?"

Folding her arms across her chest, Michelle questioned, "Is it that obvious?" She ran a nervous hand through her curls.

"It's all right, sister." He stopped an usher that was walking by them. "Sister Rollins, can you find this young lady a seat?"

The woman eyed Michelle from her head to her shoes. "I don't know where. We put anybody else in there and the fire marshal will be here."

Michelle was only too glad to leave. She found the massive cathedral intimidating. "I can just come back tomorrow."

She made a move to leave.

"Sometimes there is no tomorrow. . . ." The young man glanced around. "Put her in the usher section."

"I . . . I can sit in the balcony."

"That's exactly where we headed, child," the usher shot back.

Michelle followed the woman through the doors and up the stairs.

Bishop Jakes's words floated upward. "If there were only one thing that we should be preoccupied with praying for as it relates to our personal lives that would make you able to burn your 'wish' list, your 'gimmie' list, your 'I want more' list, your 'I need' list, and just summarize them all into one thing . . . if you would just ask God for favor, you would absolutely have it all. Better than riches, better than gold, better than notoriety. To just have favor is a powerful thing."

Michelle found an empty seat and sat down. Her purse fell, the contents spilling everywhere.

The usher bent to help her retrieve her items.

Michelle didn't miss the soft gasp that escaped the woman when she glimpsed the LoJack adorning her ankle.

Her eyes traveled upward, landing briefly on the prison tattoo on Michelle's arm.

"Did you take a Bible?" the usher inquired.

Rolling her eyes, Michelle stated, *"I didn't take nothin'!* You better get out my face."

After giving her a curious look, the usher moved on to the next person. "Did you take a Bible, Mother?"

The elderly woman responded with a smile, "Yes, I got one, baby. Thank you."

It wasn't until Michelle noticed the stack of Bibles on the floor nearby that she realized they were free for the taking.

Ashamed of the way she reacted and feeling like a heel, Michelle averted her eyes from the usher.

Every now and then, her gaze would travel the length of the sanctuary, pausing to stop on the man onstage talking.

"The Bible said, Noah, Ruth, David, Sampson, even Jesus found favor in the eyes of God. Yet most of us live with a sense of timidity and insecurity, uncertain as to whether we actually have favor or not. We gather in the arena of life like spectators, if not cheerleaders, to cheer on those that we perceive to have favor.

Never really recognizing that we, in fact, have within our own spirits, the favor of God. But like the people of the Bible, if you don't find it, you'll never be able to embrace it and unleash it in your life."

Michelle continued to survey the church. She couldn't get over how huge it was. She'd never ever been in a church this size.

She looked around, searching for Twana. Michelle spotted her seated two rows ahead of her on the other side.

A smile tugged at her lips. Twana was garbed in an outlandish pink "church lady" hat and a dress of the same color that looked as if it had been spray painted on her.

Who she think she foolin'? Michelle wondered.

When Twana started looking around, Michelle held up her hand, trying in vain to get her attention.

Cassey and Reggie had been sniping at each other the entire drive over to the church.

She sat on the passenger side staring out the window, playing with the narrow gold band on the ring finger of her left hand—a necessity in order to pull off her masquerade. Cassey wanted everyone at church to assume she and Reggie were married. She figured this way she didn't have to outright tell a lie—people would see the ring and assume what they would.

She had hoped and prayed that one day Reggie would marry her, but now it seemed as if that day would never come.

When she got saved a few years back, Cassey tried to pressure Reggie into marriage, but he never got around to divorcing his wife, despite the fact that he'd been living with Cassey over fifteen years.

Cassey took her mind off what might not ever happen because she didn't want to be left in a bad mood for revival.

"What time you gettin' off work?" Reggie demanded when they arrived at the church. He shifted the gear into Park, and then turned to face her. "Don't have me waitin' out here like last time."

Cassey sighed in frustration. "I told you already that wasn't my fault, Reggie. When church service runs over, it just runs over. I *have* to stay until the end."

He lit up a cigarette. "I need some money."

"Tomorrow is payday. All I got is my tithe money and that belongs to God."

Reggie's face went grim. "What He gonna buy with it? He God."

"That's blasphemy." Cassey's expression was tight with strain. "And Reggie, you know you don't need to be smoking."

"Look," he yelled. "I'm a grown man! Don't be telling me what *not* to smoke."

Cassey didn't respond to his words. Instead, she touched his hand and said softly, "Reggie, Michelle is gonna be here tonight. I was thinking . . . maybe after revival, she could come to the house and—"

Scowling, Reggie cut her off. "No. That convict ain't allowed in *my* house." Reggie sneered. "The way she disrespects me. I don't want her nowhere near me. Ain't no way I can feel safe in the house with her there. It ain't gon' work, Cassey. A man need to feel safe in his own home."

Cassey looked away. The misery of all that had happened still haunted her. "Michelle been in prison three years. They wouldn't be lettin' her out if she hadn't changed her life."

"People don't change. They just change folk around them."

She gave Reggie a pleading look. "Michelle's just had such a hard time in life. I'd just like to try to make some of it up to her."

"Humph. You need to be making something up to me," Reggie fumed. "Ever since you had that stroke you ain't been half the woman I need."

"You trying to hurt me?"

Reggie silenced her with a critical squint. "If I was, your paralyzed butt probably couldn't feel it. You need to be good to me. Who else would stay with you?"

His cruel words had the intended effect. Cassey reached into her purse and pulled out her offering envelope.

Ripping it open, she took out the cash and handed it to him. "Here. Just take the money."

She climbed out of the car and marched toward the steps of the cathedral.

"Don't be late either," he shouted before driving off.

Cassey gave a tiny smile at the two women lingering outside the church. She hoped that they hadn't overheard her conversation with Reggie. She'd worked hard to keep her private life away from the scrutiny of her church family.

If it had been up to her, she and Reggie would've married a long time ago. There were days when she couldn't figure out why she stayed with him—on other days, those days when he wasn't drinking, he could be so sweet and loving.

Then there was this rift between Michelle and Reggie. Their feud had been going on for years now and was wearing on Cassey's nerves.

"Michelle's just jealous of our relationship," Reggie would tell her. "That's why she's telling you all those lies. She just trying to cause trouble between us."

Cassey closed her eyes in an effort to stifle the pain. She loved her daughter. She loved Reggie. She didn't want to have to choose between the two of them.

My daughter's out of prison and my man don't even want her to come home. What am I supposed to tell her?

Bishop Jakes eyed the crowd. "Let's practice this today by just looking at somebody and telling them, 'I am highly favored.'"

The woman sitting next to Michelle uttered, "I am highly favored. . . ."

Michelle tried not to turn up her nose at the homeless woman with no teeth and matted hair.

Who was she kidding? People like them were forgotten by God, she thought sullenly. *If God loved us, she wouldn't be homeless and I wouldn't have been molested by those jerks Reggie and Pervis.*

"Tell them, 'I may not look favored. I may not feel favored. I may not seem favored . . .'"

"I may not look favored . . . ," the woman repeated.

Michelle put a hand to her face, partially covering her nose and mouth. Right now, she wanted to be anyplace but in that massive church and especially beside this homeless woman.

Twana caught her eye and gestured to show that she'd saved a seat for her. Releasing a sigh of relief, Michelle propelled her body out of the chair.

"But I am highly favored."

The homeless woman tugged on Michelle's dress to get her attention.

"But I am highly favored. . . ."

"Yes, I know you are, now let me go before you get knocked out," Michelle threatened in a low voice.

Stunned, the woman snatched her hand away.

Michelle squeezed into the row where Twana was sitting. "I'm so glad to get away from up there. That lady stank."

Bishop Jakes's words caught her attention.

"'My circumstances may not look favored. My bank account may not look favored. But I am favored. . . .' Demons tremble when you talk like that. The Lord favors you. If God kisses you, who can curse you?"

Michelle's eyes strayed back to where the homeless lady was sitting.

"I'm glad you made it," Twana whispered as she reached over and squeezed Michelle's hand.

"These young girls today are just too fast," Twana gossiped. "Look at Elder Smith's daughter over there tryin' to look all innocent. You know she expecting. She ain't got no husband either."

A woman sitting behind them leaned over Twana's shoulder.

"Twana, where did you get your weave? Mine itches me."

Twana shook her head. "Some people that call themselves church folk need to mind their own business. . . . These folks too much for me. Do you believe this, Michelle?"

Michelle hid her grin behind her hand.

"Touch somebody and tell them that I'm glad I'm sitting by you tonight," Bishop Jakes instructed.

Twana and Michelle looked toward one another. "I'm glad I'm sitting by you tonight," they said in unison.

Michelle struggled to keep her attention focused on Bishop Jakes's sermon. She glanced around the sanctuary looking for Cassey.

Twana nudged Michelle hard. "Is that Dark Gable, Brown Sugar or Sweet Molasses over there?"

Michelle followed her gaze to Todd, who was standing a few feet away.

"Girl, if you don't get on that man, I'm just gon' have to rob the cradle."

She pretended not to be interested, asking Twana instead, "Where does Cassey sit?"

"She's working selling ministry merchandise this week, so she'll be out front."

"Oh."

Gesturing to get Todd's attention, Twana uttered, "I'll go find her, let Todd save my seat."

Twana sashayed over to Todd and whispered something in his ear.

Michelle's heart began to beat faster as Todd headed over to join her.

Smiling, he sat down.

"Don't be intimidated if you don't feel favored," Bishop Jakes told the crowd. "Because favor has to father you. It has to mentor you. It has to develop you. It has to train you. If favor released everything that it has for you now, you wouldn't be able to stand it."

Stealing glances at Todd, Michelle couldn't deny he looked extremely handsome in his suit. Her heart did a little flip.

". . . Favor has to wean you from the dependency on your support systems. Break you away from needing the approval of your generation. Favor has to take you through controversy until you can learn how to stand on your own two feet. Favor has to isolate you so that it can integrate you into God's divine purpose for your life. Favor has to take you through loneliness and prove you, and propel you and then release you into your destiny. I'm telling you that God's had you in boot camp for the last few years getting you ready to go to the front line."

Applause and shouts of "Praise Him" and "Hallelujah" erupted all over the sanctuary.

Michelle's mind was no longer on anything Bishop Jakes said. Right now she was thinking of all the things she wanted to do to Todd.

He scanned her critically and beamed approval. "Michelle . . . you, uh . . ."

"Clean up pretty well?" she finished for him. She let her gaze take him in. "I could say the same about you."

He stared with longing at her. "I don't think I ever want to leave this seat."

She chuckled. "That's one way to join the church."

"You busy afterward?"

"Hardly . . . why?"

"I was hoping we could get a cup of coffee or something."

Every time Todd's gaze met hers, Michelle's heart turned over in response. "I can do coffee."

"I don't really drink coffee but I'll sip on hot water with you, if you let me."

Michelle laughed.

The woman sitting beside her leaned over and said in a stern whisper, "Some of us came here to hear the sermon."

"Sorry," Todd whispered back.

Blushing, Michelle turned her attention to the pulpit. She fought her overwhelming need to be close to him and forced her impure thoughts to the back of her mind. She sat with her fingers lost in the folds of her dress, listening to Bishop Jakes's sermon.

"Favor gave Joseph a dream of moving into a position of power and authority. And then threw him in a pit to father him, prepare him, train him, mentor him, tutor him, develop him . . ."

She could feel Todd's eyes on her, the heat of his gaze sending warmth through her. Michelle clenched her hands into fists, resisting the urge to stroke his cheek the way she used to when they were younger.

Michelle pushed her attention back to Bishop Jakes, who was saying, "When you're really favored, you'll get a word that's up and a situation that's down. When you're really favored, your whole life is a contradiction. How can things be so right and still be so wrong? How can I know my favor while my wounds bleed? Remember, favor uses tragedy to birth greatness. Joseph was sold into slavery, but this led to his destiny. You can't do anything to somebody favored that won't be turned into a testimony."

She could relate to some of what he was saying. Her life was one filled with tragedy. From the moment she lost her childhood, Michelle spiraled downward through the rest of her life. But she found it hard to believe that anything good, much less great, could come from the mess that was her life.

"You know your daughter's in here," Twana announced as she sauntered up to Cassey's table in the lobby area of the cathedral. Her words carried a strong suggestion of reproach.

Standing in front of the table, Twana pulled on her dress, trying to keep it from crawling up her thighs.

Cassey made sure the cassette tapes were displayed neatly before responding, "It's because of me that she's here."

Playing with the strap of her purse, Twana countered, "I could say *Amen* for six or seven reasons."

Cassey's gaze met hers. Keeping her voice low, she uttered, "Reggie don't want her around. Those two are like oil and water." She glanced around the lobby, then released a long sigh before muttering, "I just want some peace in my house."

Twana leaned forward. "Ever wonder why they don't get along?"

Glancing around to see if anyone was listening, Cassey ground out between clenched teeth, "This ain't the place for this, Twana."

"What is the place then?" Twana demanded. Her tone harsh, she asked, "You gonna let that man continue to keep you from your child? I wouldn't let no man keep me from my own flesh and blood."

"Reggie ain't doing nothing," Cassey stated in a choked voice.

"I'm just keeping the peace. In case you forgot, Twana . . . Michelle ain't so squeaky clean herself, you know. She the one on probation—*not Reggie*. He's the victim."

"Humph. Quite an injustice, if you ask me. You know why she went to prison in the first place? That don't put some questions in your mind, Cassey? It sho' does mine."

In spite of Cassey's reserve, a tingle of exasperation came into her voice. "Twana, I love you dearly . . . but remember that all my business is none of yours."

Straightening the hat on her head, Twana glared at Cassey. "You better be glad I'm saved."

"Humph," Cassey grunted.

Twana held back. This was not the place to give her friend the tongue-lashing she so desperately deserved. "What you doin' . . . the way you treatin' Michelle . . . it ain't right. You and I need to have a long talk, Cassey."

Cassey's mouth dipped into a deep frown. "Not if it's about what goes on in my house, we don't."

"One day you gon' regret how you treated your own child," Twana retorted. "Just wait and see."

"You don't know what you talkin' 'bout. Just stay out my business." Cassey's eyes surveyed the area, making sure nobody was listening to them. "This conversation is over."

Without another word, Twana walked, head held high, back into the sanctuary.

Cassey was her best friend, but there were times she just wanted to strangle the woman. What in the world did she see in that snake anyway?

Twana knew the answer to that. Back in the day, it was all

Cassey could talk about. But where was he when she had that stroke? Out with his friends doing who knows what. She was the one who Cassey called to take her to the hospital. And Michelle. What he did to that girl . . .

Twana wanted so much to take away the pain in her god-daughter's life. Michelle was her baby, too. The closest she would ever get to having a child of her own.

Maybe I'm not the best person. The Lord knows I've done my share of sinning. I can't take away the past, but oh how I wish I could help that poor girl.

She released a calming breath. No, she couldn't erase the past, but she could ask for God's forgiveness and blessing so that she might be there for Michelle.

Closing her eyes, Twana sent up a silent prayer. *Father God, my heart is torn apart. I have no strength left in me and no consolation in my heart. I cry to You for help, Father. The Bible says that the Lord is near to those who have a broken heart, and saves such who have a contrite spirit. I ask that You comfort me, Lord, because all my dreams are shattered. My hope is lost and I find total darkness in front of me. Lord, lead me by Your Spirit into deeper spiritual experiences and make my life a fruitful one. Guide me so that I might assist Michelle and lead her to You. Thank You, Father, for being with me during these hard times and for Your assurances of joy and peace. Amen.*

When Twana opened her eyes, she felt better. She pulled a tissue from her purse and wiped her eyes.

She nodded and began clapping her hands at Bishop Jakes's words. "Amen," she uttered in agreement. "That's right. Tell it. . . ."

Outside in the lobby area, Cassey discreetly brushed away an escaping tear with the back of her hand.

"Lord, my nerves are raw," she whispered beneath her breath.

She fumbled with the tapes to keep her mind off the conversation she'd had with Twana. *I'm sitting here crying for nothing. I did the best I could for Michelle. I got nothing to be guilty of. . . . If only Michelle had put forth more effort to get along with Reggie.*

He's not exactly blameless, she admitted. *Reggie could've tried harder, too.*

Cassey's troubled thoughts were devoured by the thundering sound of people filing out of the sanctuary. Surveying the crowd of churchgoers, she stood up to search out her daughter.

After a while, she spotted Michelle standing a few feet away with Todd.

Cassey placed a hand to her mouth and called out to her, waving to get Michelle's attention.

Her daughter stopped walking at the sound of her name and turned around. "Cassey . . ."

"Over here."

Michelle whispered something to Todd before walking over to her.

Cassey's arms ached to hold her daughter, but something in Michelle's eyes stopped her. She pasted on a smile and said, "You made it."

"Yeah, I made it. Not like I had any real choice in the matter."

"You . . . you look well."

Michelle didn't respond. She glanced over her shoulder.

Cassey took a deep breath and adjusted her smile. "We got a lot of reacquainting to do. We need to have some uninterrupted mother-daughter time. What you think 'bout that?"

Michelle shrugged.

"It'll be good. We need to just sit down and talk to each other."

"If you say so."

Cassey sighed in resignation. "Michelle, I'm trying. You got to meet me halfway."

Michelle gave her mother a cold look. "I don't have to do anything for you. What have you done for me?"

"I don't want to argue with you," Cassey whispered. "Now you really should be grateful. I was the one that got you here."

"What did you bring me back for?" Michelle asked. "It's not like you really want me around."

Her eyes traveled slowly over her mother's face. There was something wrong. Michelle squinted. "Cassey . . . your face. What's different about it?"

She turned away, but Michelle took a step closer. "What happened to your face?"

Cassey waved her hand in dismissal. "A little Bell's palsy . . . just stress."

Concerned, Michelle's eyes moved down to Cassey's twisted hand. "In your hand, too? Did you have a . . . a stroke?"

Cassey gave a slight nod. "Two years ago. Very slight. I'm fine."

A flicker of apprehension coursed through her. Michelle wondered if Reggie was treating her mother well. Had he been her caretaker during her recovery period?

"Oooh Cassey . . ." A wave of guilt flowed through her over the way she had just talked to her mother.

"I'm fine," Cassey assured her. "I know you don't believe me, but it's the truth. I'm so glad to see you, Michelle. We have so much to talk about. This is our chance to start over."

Within Michelle, a spark of hope ignited. "I . . ."

Outside the church, they heard the sound of a car horn blow. "Excuse me," Cassey murmured before walking over to the glass door and peeking out.

Over her shoulder, she told Michelle, "I'm sorry, but I gotta go. Why don't we try to get together sometime tomorrow? That'll be better."

Michelle refused to allow her mother to see how hurt and rejected she felt. She vowed a long time ago never to let Cassey view her heartbreak.

Cassey walked briskly out the exit doors, leaving Michelle behind.

This is the way it's always been, she told herself. *Nothing mattered to my mother except having a man by her side. Not even a daughter who loved her unconditionally.*

Twana walked over to her. "Where did Cassey go?"

"To Reggie," Michelle stated dryly. "Where else would she go?"

Her godmother gave her a sympathetic smile. "Well, did you at least get a chance to talk to her?"

Michelle shook her head no. "I need to get going. Thanks for the dress and everything, Twana."

Todd walked over to where they were standing. "You ready to go?"

"I'm ready," she told him. "See you, Twana."

A flash of merriment crossed Twana's face. "Y'all have fun."

Michelle shot Twana a bland look over her shoulder.

Twana grinned, her eyes full of mischief.

"How did it go?" Todd inquired as they headed out of the church to the car.

Michelle was so caught up in her thoughts that she didn't hear him.

"Hey you," he prompted.

She glanced in his direction. "What?"

"With your mom. Everything go all right?"

Michelle released a long sigh. "I don't feel like talkin' about it. Let's just go, Todd."

7

Inside the prison cell, Michelle changed her position by uncrossing her legs and stretching them out. Her legs were starting to cramp, so she rubbed her thighs gently.

After a moment, she returned her attention to the tiny matchstick house she was working on.

"It wasn't the first time she chose him over me, Bishop," Michelle stated as she worked. "She was always choosing men over her daughter. I was just an inconvenience to her."

"You don't really believe that, do you, Michelle?" Bishop Jakes wanted to know.

She met his gaze straight on. "Yeah, I do."

"After all these years, it must have been a little uncomfortable for her. For both of you. Like two familiar strangers."

Michelle shot Bishop Jakes a penetrating look. "Sometimes you have to choose between the devil you know and the daughter you don't."

She picked up a matchstick and held it up to the dim lighting in her cell, examining it. Satisfied, Michelle applied a thin layer of glue and stuck it on the tiny house.

"Don't you think your mom wishes she could have made some different choices?"

"She *made* her choices all right," Michelle reflected with some bitterness. "She ain't changed to this day. After everything that's happened, she still ain't changed."

Michelle looked up at him. "You know, I actually thought it would be different when I got out of prison. I thought maybe those three years made her think about things, too. I shoulda known better."

Michelle shook her head and went back to her work. "You know what they say, 'Expect nothin' and you won't be disappointed.'"

"I imagine your mother thought things could be different, too, Michelle. When she came to me, asking me to petition for your early parole, she really believed revival would turn things around for you. Her dream was that it would be the first step toward healing your relationship."

"Dream? Please, Bishop. People like me ain't got no right to dreams. I learned that a long time ago. Had good teachers. My dreams died thirteen years ago; now all I got are nightmares."

1991

"We're gonna be the most famous singers in the world," Michelle told her doll. "We're gonna be stars. Now you sing backup and I'm singing the lead. Think you can handle that, Gigi?"

"Sure," she answered in a squeaky voice for the doll.

Holding the doll up like a microphone, she began, "Ladies and gentlemen . . . Michelle Jordan and Gigi. . . ."

She pranced around the room, singing.

Suddenly, Reggie burst through the door, bringing her singing to a halt and triggering alarm bells in her brain.

She hid the doll behind her back.

"Where's your mama?"

"Said she was going downtown to pay a bill. . . ." Michelle could feel the heat of his gaze roaming up and down her body, prompting her to add, "But she'll be right back." Her eyes skimmed the top of his shoes. He'd been drinking—she could smell it on his breath. She hated when he was like this. There were times when Uncle Reggie was real nice to her but that was mostly in the beginning. Then after that, he was nice when he hadn't been drinking. He didn't yell at her like Cassey did, and he would sneak treats to her room, small rewards for her accomplishments. But when he came home drunk, he was as scary as any monster Michelle ever imagined.

"Ain't it about time you stopped playing with dolls?"

Michelle kept her eyes glued to the floor and didn't respond.

"Look at me when I talk to you."

Michelle glanced upward, her body trembling in fear. He had

that look in his eye again. It made her feel dirty, although she couldn't explain why.

"How long you wanna stay a kid?"

"I . . . I don't kn-know." She inched toward her room, hoping to escape. Once she made it safely to her bedroom, she would lock the door.

Michelle took a step back.

Reggie grabbed her by the arm. "Where you going?" he demanded.

She held her doll close to her chest. "My baby is ready to go to bed."

"Is she now? Well, everybody in this house gotta kiss me good night first."

Fear swirled around in her stomach, making her nauseous. Swallowing hard, Michelle moved to step around him. "She ain't allowed."

Surprising her, Reggie snatched the doll from the safety of her arms. He kissed it before handing it back to Michelle.

"I think your baby liked it. She's still smiling."

Michelle prayed for her mother's swift return home. "Well, I'm not ready to go to bed yet."

She played with the ribbon on her favorite dress. "I gotta change outta my school clothes. Cassey's gon' be upset if I have them on when she gets home. She'll be here any minute."

Michelle made a second attempt to get by him, but Reggie thwarted her efforts.

"Well, just give me a kiss and then you can go."

She was disgusted by his request. Cassey might like kissing him, but Michelle found the very idea revolting. She'd long since figured out Uncle Reggie wasn't really her uncle. Right when he moved into their house and into her mother's bedroom.

"My mama don't like me to play in my school clothes. She's gonna be mad."

"Then you need to hurry up."

Reggie bent down and extended his cheek. "C'mon now."

Fighting nausea, Michelle closed her eyes and moved to give him a quick peck on the cheek. She hoped he would leave her alone afterward.

He turned his head, covering her lips with his.

Horrified and humiliated, Michelle pushed away from him.

He laughed. "See? That wasn't so bad. I see a little smile on your face, too."

Michelle dropped her eyes to the floor. "I got to change my clothes before my mama gets home."

Nodding, Reggie stepped aside. "Go ahead and change then."

Relieved, Michelle walked briskly toward her room.

"Hey, Michelle," Reggie called out suddenly. "I'm even gonna help you."

Before she could protest, he'd swooped her up in his arms and was carrying her toward the bedroom.

"Put me down, Uncle Reggie!" Michelle screamed in terror. "Put me down!"

"You always around here teasing me, with your little tight jeans on. I'm gonna see if you're ready."

Panicking, Michelle screamed. "Please stop. . . . Mama. . . . Stop him. . . ."

"Don't be calling yo' mama now. . . . You ought not be so fast around me. I'm a man. You doing all that teasing . . . I'ma give you what you been asking for."

. . .

Michelle's pain-wracked body wouldn't stop trembling, nor did the burning sensation between her legs dissipate. She lay on damp sheets stained with her tears, blood and vomit.

She moaned and tried to move, but shock held her immobile. "Mama . . . ," she whimpered.

Michelle bit her bottom lip until it throbbed and found the will to sit up gingerly in bed. *I want my mama,* she screamed in her mind. Fear tore at her heart—fear that Uncle Reggie would return before her mother came home.

Ignoring the pain, Michelle sobbed as she searched for a place to hide. She couldn't let Uncle Reggie hurt her again. She couldn't understand what she'd done. She never teased him like he accused her of doing. She didn't much talk to him at all.

Michelle went from room to room, looking for the perfect place to hide from Uncle Reggie. She glanced down at her bloody dress.

It was ruined.

Mama's gon' be so mad at me. She shook her head no. I'm gon' tell her what Uncle Reggie did—she'll be mad with him.

In the kitchen, she found the perfect place to stay until her mother came home. Michelle crouched down, receiving a flash of pain for her efforts. She gulped hard, hot tears slipping down her cheeks.

Michelle yielded to the compulsive sobs that shook her. She was so afraid—more afraid than she'd ever been in her life. Although she cried because of the pain, her sense of loss was beyond tears.

The image of Reggie hurling nasty words, slobbering on her

and holding her down against her will, infiltrated Michelle's mind, triggering another round of sobs.

What did I do? Michelle wondered wildly as she fought another bout of nausea. *What did I do to him? Why did this happen to me?*

Weary, Cassey trudged into her house. She was so glad to be home . . . until she opened the door. She stood there, shaking her head, surveying the wreck that was once her living room.

She spied an empty vodka bottle and frowned.

Reggie had been drinking again.

Cassey hated when he got drunk because he wasn't a nice person. A few times he'd even gotten violent with her. She'd put him out after the third time, but allowed him to come back a week later after he promised never to hit her again.

"Reggie?"

No answer.

She called out for him a second time.

He was probably stretched out on her brand-new comforter in their bedroom. "He bet' not have his stinking feet all over my stuff," she fussed.

The bedroom was empty.

Cassey searched around the rest of the house looking for him.

"That messy excuse for a man. I don't know why I keep putting up with him," she muttered. She was getting sick and tired of picking up after him.

In the beginning he was everything she'd ever dreamed of—that's why she let him move in. Reggie made her feel loved. He'd made her feel special. But she soon discovered that he didn't want to get a job—he was content living off her.

He'd cheated on her, abused her mentally and physically, but even then, Cassey couldn't let him go. She didn't want him to leave her because she didn't want to be alone. Anything was better than sleeping in a bed alone night after night.

"Michelle?" she called out.

Cassey marched down the hall to her daughter's bedroom.

She paused long enough to pick up the star that had fallen from her door. "I don't know why you want this fool thing hanging on here anyway," she muttered. "Like you some Hollywood star . . . humph."

She flung it carelessly to the side.

When Cassey opened the door to her daughter's room, her eyes stretched wide open. "No you didn't. Look at this bed . . . Michelle! I'm gonna beat the black off that behind."

Michelle knew better than to leave her room looking like this. The child had lost her mind.

Fuming, Cassey strode back into the living room.

A soft whimpering caught her attention. She stood still and listened, trying to determine where it was coming from.

The kitchen.

Cassey walked into the kitchen, saying, "Oh, you just wait . . . Mmm-hmmmm . . . I'm gonna show you how I am not to be played with."

Cassey opened the top drawer and removed an ironing cord. She raised her arm with the cord poised in the air, ready to strike, and flung open the closet door.

Shocked, Cassey dropped the cord.

Michelle sat wrapped in a bloodstained sheet, weeping uncontrollably.

"Michelle? What you crying about?"

Her daughter moved the sheet in front of her to reveal that the bottom of her dress was wet from the blood.

"Did you get your period? I told you you would get your visitor one day, didn't I? Ain't nothing to cry about. Get on up."

"H-he . . . he h-hurt me, Mommy. . . ."

It took her a split second to comprehend what Michelle was saying to her, but Cassey couldn't handle the brutal truth. Shaking her head, she asked, "What? Michelle, what you talkin' 'bout, girl?"

Her daughter repeated her words.

Cassey grabbed her by the shoulders. "Who hurt you? What you talking about?"

"He p-pushed . . . held me d-down . . ."

She pretended not to understand. The implication was just too dreadful. Cassey felt sick to her stomach. "What you saying, girl?"

"He hurt me, Mommy. He hurt m me."

A look of horror washed over Cassey's face, prompting Michelle to whisper, "I'm sorry."

"Who you let in the house?" she inquired. "That lil' niggah down the street I see you talking to all the time? I told you that you was getting too fast for your own good."

She shook her head.

"Reggie kept trying to tell me, but I wouldn't listen. . . ."

Michelle reached for her mother. She needed to feel Cassey's arms around her. She wanted her mother to make Reggie leave and never come back.

"I told you 'bout messing around with that niggah down the street."

Michelle searched for a way to make Cassey understand. "No . . . Mama. I-it was R-Reggie. . . ."

Shock rushed through Cassey's body. "What you say?" Putting her hand on her hips, she stood toe-to-toe with Michelle. "What did you say? How you just gonna lie like that? You let that boy do anything he want to you and since it ain't what you bargained for—you gonna lie on Reggie?"

Michelle cowered and raised her hands to ward off an attack.

Her mother didn't hit her, but she might as well have done so—the results were just as devastating to Michelle.

Shaking her head in disbelief, Cassey continued, "Nah, this here is yo' fault. You shouldn't have let this happen! And if you keep on with your fast behind, I'ma send you to your grandma. You mess around and get yo'self a baby—you can't live here."

Michelle couldn't move. Baby? Another wave of fear spread through her body. She didn't want a baby.

Her eyes dropped down to the blood-splattered dress, then back up to Cassey's face. "M-my d-dress . . ."

"Get on in that bathroom and clean yo'self up. You gonna stay with Twana tonight. And don't you go over there telling Twana those lies. You better keep yo' mouth shut. I mean it. 'Cause if I hear anything, you gon' really be sorry. What goes on in this house better stay in this house."

Michelle flinched from her mother's words.

"You hear me?"

"Yes ma'am," she whispered.

"Now get out my face. Go in your room and put on some clean clothes. Don't forget to wash yo' nasty butt. I can't believe you putting me through all this mess. You ought to be ashamed of yo'self."

Michelle tuned out the rest of Cassey's rantings because the words were just too painful. Her body still felt as if it had been ripped to pieces, but that pain didn't compare to the way her mother had shredded her fragile emotions.

Her eyes spotted the star that once hung on her door.

It had been kicked off to the side, lying in a forgotten corner. For her, it no longer held the promise of a dream come true.

Tears in her eyes, Michelle picked it up and tossed it in a nearby trash can.

Later, she stood beneath running water, trying to rid herself of the unclean feeling—the feel of Reggie's filthy hands all over her body. Michelle's tears blended with the water from the showerhead.

That night, before her mother took her to Twana's, Michelle crept outside, carrying her ruined dress.

In the backyard, she buried it beneath the huge tree where an old swing used to hang.

Unlike her mother, she couldn't just cast it away—this burden. It would stay with her forever.

She would never be the same.

8

Michelle closed her eyes and shook her head to ward off the painful memory.

"He didn't just take my innocence that day, Bishop. Reggie took my hope. He took my mother." She swallowed hard, trying not to reveal her anger.

"Can you believe that? My own mama stood there and accused me of lying 'bout what happened. What you do, Bishop, when your whole world seems to be crumbling down around you?"

"You don't give up," he replied.

She gave him a wry smile. "I thought you'd say something corny like that."

"You survived to get this far."

She nodded. "Oh, I survived all right."

Michelle sat silent for a moment.

"After the abuse, I felt completely ashamed of even being alive."

Her eyes traveled to Bishop Jakes. "I managed to bury these feelings in order to survive and live my life."

Michelle broke into a short laugh. "Look at me, Bishop. I'm here sitting in a jail cell. What the heck am I surviving?"

"Michelle, you can't give up now," Bishop Jakes said softly.

"Why not?" she snapped. "I told you things don't change."

She let out a sigh and continued, almost pleading, "Look, Bishop, I am what I am. I was destined for this life. It was my birthright. A legacy of pain . . . that's all I got."

"Michelle . . ." Twana's voice died at the sight of the little girl when she opened her front door. Her eyes were swollen from crying and the poor thing stood there trembling.

Twana looked up to see Cassey's car pull away, then she turned her attention back to Michelle. "What on earth is the matter, baby girl?"

"M-Mama want me to stay with you."

"Honey, come on in this house," Twana urged.

Her heart nearly stopped beating when she noted the way Michelle was walking. Twana struggled to keep her composure. Something wasn't right.

"Take a seat. I was gonna—" She stopped short when Michelle didn't plop down like she usually did—instead, she eased down as if . . . as if . . .

Twana rushed to Michelle's side and hugged her close. "Oooh baby girl . . . ," she murmured over and over. "I'm so sorry."

After a moment, she asked, "Do you wanna tell me what happened to you, baby?" Deep down, Twana already had some idea.

Michelle shook her head.

"Honey, now you know you can tell your godmother anything."

"Mama . . ." Michelle began to cry. "She . . . she gon' whup me. . . ."

Twana calmed her fears. "Don't you worry 'bout your mama. She not gon' bother you—not as long as I have breath in my body." Anger flashed in her eyes. "I should go over there and kill that snake," Twana muttered under her breath. "I never liked that Reggie. Never did."

She pulled away from Michelle gently. Twana stroked her cheek and said, "I'm gonna make you a nice bubble bath."

"Mama made me wash—"

Twana cut her off. "Honey, I'm gonna wash you so clean that you're gonna give Snow White some competition."

She took Michelle's hand and smiled. "Then we're gon' have us some of my famous chicken noodle soup. I just made up a batch yesterday. That sound good to you?"

Michelle nodded.

"A bowl of chicken noodle soup will make us feel better. It won't chase away the demons, but it will help for tonight."

Reaching out, Michelle embraced Twana.

Stroking her back, Twana promised, "Honey, it's gon' be all right."

"I love you, Twana."

"Baby girl, I love you, too."

They pulled apart.

Wiping her eyes, Twana uttered, "Let's get you into that bath."

Michelle followed her down the hall, relieved that she didn't have to tell Twana anything—she'd figured it out all by herself. Cassey would still accuse her of telling though.

She hated her mother right now. Cassey had been so mean to her. Michelle watched in silence as Twana filled the tub with water.

"This is a lavender scent . . . ," she was saying, pouring some oil into the tub.

"You're gon' love this, Michelle." Twana glanced over her shoulder. "Take off your clothes, honey."

Michelle felt a wave of shame and embarrassment wash over her. She hesitated.

Twana sat down on the edge of the bathtub. "I saw you before you saw yourself. Baby girl, I used to change your nasty diapers. Go on and take off those clothes." Standing up, she added, "I bought you some brand-new pajamas last weekend. I'll go get them."

Michelle took off her clothes and climbed into the tub. The heat from the water was soothing to the tender flesh between her legs.

Twana reentered the bathroom, saying, "Tomorrow, we're going shopping. I'ma buy you some new clothes."

Michelle smiled for the first time since arriving.

Twana hummed as she bathed her. Her gentle touch mixed with the warm water soothed Michelle's aching body.

"Let me get you out this water before you start looking like a raisin."

Twana picked a huge fluffy towel and held it open for Michelle.

Michelle climbed out and allowed her godmother to dry her off. Twana's touch was soft and caring.

"Put on some of this lavender-scented lotion, baby girl. While you getting dressed, I'ma fix the soup."

"Thank you, Twana."

A tear slipped down Michelle's cheek and Twana sighed in resignation, hugging her again. "Oooh honey."

Michelle wished Twana was her mother. She just wished she had a mother, 'cause tonight she felt like she didn't have one at all. A mother is supposed to love you, protect you.

She would never really think of Cassey as her mother again.

A string of curses fell from Reggie's mouth.

He tried to still his trembling hand long enough to take a puff of his cigarette.

It was all Michelle's fault.

She just kept on sashaying and enticing him—the looks she gave him; Reggie was powerless to resist. He was a man, after all. A man was only so strong. Besides, the little girl really needed to be taught a lesson.

Reggie tried to clear his head by drinking a cup of coffee. He'd promised Cassey he wouldn't drink as much as he had in the past. He'd been sneaking around behind her back for a while, buying liquor, and was tired of trying to keep it away from her.

He'd planned on just going home and sleeping it off, but then he saw Michelle. She looked so pretty in that little pink-and-white dress. It fit her budding body like a glove.

Michelle was only twelve but she had the body of a teenager. She was already curvy like Cassey.

Reggie glanced around the bar, eyeing the other customers talking, laughing and drinking around him.

A woman winked at him as she passed by.

He smiled and then looked away.

Right now, Reggie wasn't interested in flirting—he was more worried over how Cassey was gonna react.

That lil' blabbermouth ain't gonna keep her mouth shut, he thought angrily.

Recalling how he'd left the house, he groaned inwardly. He should've tried to straighten up before he left, but afterward, Reggie couldn't stay another minute in that house. He had to get away.

Michelle was bawling like he'd . . .

Reggie shook his head in denial. She asked for it. Michelle was always asking for it.

Cassey . . . would she believe Michelle or could he convince her that her daughter was a liar? Could he wrangle himself out of this mess?

Reggie wasn't so sure.

He consoled himself with the fact that Cassey was a desperate, lonely woman. All he had to do was threaten to leave her. He knew how to make her feel stupid for doubting him. He would just play on her insecurities, Reggie decided.

He glanced up at a clock hanging on the wall in the bar. It was still too early to go home.

"I need another cup of coffee," he grunted.

His hands were no longer trembling.

Reggie eyed a young woman sitting a couple of chairs away from him. Catching her eye, he smiled.

The woman gave Reggie a haughty look and turned away.

Cursing, he turned his attention back to the cup of coffee in front of him.

Reggie took a sip and frowned.

He really wanted a drink, but he had to have his wits about him when he saw Cassey.

Cassey. He was gonna have a big fight on his hands. Reggie struggled to think of what he was going to say to her.

I was good to Michelle, he mused silently. I was better to her than her own mother. I talked to her; listened to her—even gave her gifts. . . .

Memories from long ago crept into Reggie's mind uninvited.

Images of him as a child and his caretaker.

Reggie tried to force the troubling thoughts out of his head, but could not. They returned with a vengeance.

Reggie shook his head, attempting to unhinge the thoughts he'd fought so hard to bury. Thoughts of the woman who was supposed to be looking out for him, touching him and making him do things . . . things he didn't want to do to her.

"You know you like it," she would say to him. "In time you'll welcome it."

"I don't want to, Miss Arnett." Reggie would try to push her away. "Please don't make me do it."

"It's time you grow up. Be a man," she would scold, dragging him back into her bedroom.

Reggie wiped away the tears streaming down his face with the back of his hand.

"You okay?" the bartender asked, tearing Reggie away from the memories. "You want some more coffee?"

"Naw. Gimme a vodka, straight."

Reggie finished off his cigarette while he waited for his drink. He checked the clock again. It was still too soon to go home.

Reggie began to have second thoughts. Maybe staying out too late would work against him. It would give Cassey too much time to think about things.

He quickly downed the volka and asked for another. Reggie tossed the second one down his throat.

He got up to leave.

"Showtime . . . ," he murmured dryly.

The large kitchen knife gleamed in the stream of moonlight that infiltrated the room through the picture window.

Cassey held it in a death grip as she sat in the dark watching her front door, waiting for Reggie to come home.

How could he hurt her this way? How could he do this to Michelle—he was supposed to be a father to her.

Cassey recalled the harsh words she had spoken to her daughter. Words she could never take back.

She'd called Michelle a liar.

Now here she was sitting here waiting to confront Reggie. She didn't believe he was capable of doing something so horrible, but Cassey couldn't just ignore the question in the back of her mind. Michelle was her daughter and she had to confront Reggie.

The sound of a car pulling up outside caught her attention.

Stiffening, Cassey braced herself and steadied the knife. She waited for the familiar sounds of the lock turning.

Nothing.

After a while, Cassey fell back against the chair both disappointed and relieved.

Then she heard voices and loud laughter.

She sat up and gripped the knife tighter.

Her eyes grew wet with unshed tears as she stared down at her weapon. Reggie couldn't get away with what he'd done. Cassey knew all too well what her daughter had experienced—the same thing had happened to her. Only it was by her own flesh-and-blood daddy.

Cassey shook her head, unable to accept the fact that Reggie could have been as vile as her own father. There was no way he could do something so horrible. She simply couldn't make herself believe it.

Then why was she sitting in the dark waiting on Reggie and holding a knife? her heart questioned.

Because there was a sliver of a chance that Michelle was telling the truth. Because Reggie was a dog with a capital D.

It nearly made Cassey sick just to think about it. As sick as she felt when she went into Michelle's room and had to clean up her daughter's ruined bedsheets.

Cassey pushed back her overwhelming urge to puke as she stuffed the stained sheets in the washing machine. Even now, the stench emanating from them still burned in her nostrils.

She heard the car outside drive away and groaned in frustration. Cassey wanted to have it out with Reggie now, while she was filled with white-hot rage.

I'ma kill you, Reggie. If you did this to Michelle, I'ma have to kill you.

Her eyelids grew heavy.

Cassey looked at the clock hanging on the wall over the television. She'd been sitting in this spot for hours.

An image of Michelle formed in her mind.

Cassey entertained the idea of calling Twana to check on her daughter, but she changed her mind. She'd treated Michelle horribly. Shame poured out of her pores, filling the air.

She stretched out on her sofa and cried softly.

The sound of another car stopping in front of her house stopped her tears. Cassey sat up.

Another false alarm.

Cassey fell asleep.

A voice called to her, bringing her out of her slumber. Startled, she straightened, and tightened her grip on the knife.

"Baby, what's going on?" Reggie inquired. "Why you sleepin' in the living room?"

Cassey noted the way his eyes darted around the room. Getting to her feet, she confronted Reggie. "What did you do to Michelle?"

His eyes traveled to the knife she was holding. Cassey followed his gaze.

In a swift move, Reggie took the knife away from her.

Glaring, he responded, "I didn't do nothing to Michelle. What lie the girl tell now? All I know is, that girl been trying to come between us since I moved in and you know that."

She glared at him with burning, reproachful eyes. "Did you touch her, Reggie?"

"What? Did I . . ." His mouth dropped open in shock. "Do you know what you asking me?"

"Did you touch her?"

Cassey searched his eyes for the truth.

"I c-can't . . . I can't believe you . . . ," Reggie sputtered. "You think you ain't woman enough for me?"

"I don't know if anybody is," Cassey snarled.

"Look. I don't like how you looking at me. I didn't touch her. I ain't gotta sit here and be accused of something I didn't do. Now I don't know what went down, but you know how fast that girl been getting."

Reggie pointed at her. "You even said so yourself! No telling how many different boyfriends she got. How you gonna believe her over me? How you gonna do that?"

When Cassey didn't respond, he grumbled, "Fine. I'm packing my stuff."

Reggie stomped off to the bedroom. "And when I leave this place, I ain't coming back."

She followed him into the room after a moment.

When she entered the bedroom, Reggie was busy taking clothes out of the drawers and throwing them into an old suitcase.

"Wait."

He stopped packing.

"I'll help you," she uttered.

Cassey pulled a handful of his shirts out of a drawer and tossed them on the bed. "You sorry . . ."

Reggie grabbed her.

"Let me go," Cassey screamed.

She punched him in his chest.

He grabbed her arms, holding her tight.

"I'm sorry, Cassey. I'll leave. But you know I didn't do nothing. I ain't do nothing . . . you hear?"

Reggie let her go and resumed his packing. "And when the truth come out, you really gonna be sorry. 'Cause I'ma be long gone. As good as I been to you. I'm the best man you ever had. How you gonna try to accuse me. You was gonna stab me, too."

Shaking his head, Reggie stated, "Naw, I ain't got to take this from you or that lying child of yours . . . I don't need this kind of crap in my life. I'm outta here."

She digested every word Reggie spoke. Deep down, she wanted to believe him. "Where are you going?" Cassey asked.

"What it matter?" Reggie shot back. "I'm leaving. You gon' believe some lies that fast little girl of yours telling."

Pointing to his chest, he added, "You know what that says 'bout me? I ain't one of those sick . . ."

His eyes glistened with tears. "She a kid, Cassey. There are plenty women out there if I got to do something like that. I know that's yo' daughter, but Michelle—she fast and she a liar."

Her hands on her hips, Cassey asked one final time, "So you saying you never touched her?" She studied his face, noting his expression of hurt. If he were guilty, he wouldn't look so wounded, she told herself. Cassey saw the sheen of tears that bordered his eyes.

"Yeah, that's exactly what I'm saying." He wiped his eyes with the back of his hand. "So who you believe, Cassey? Me or Michelle?"

Still confused and unsure of the answer, Cassey stood there in silence. If Reggie was telling the truth, then it meant Michelle was lying, but if Michelle was telling the truth, then the man she loved raped her daughter.

Reggie sighed before walking over to the closet, where he removed another armload of shirts.

I can't let him leave, her heart whispered. I don't want to be alone. Maybe Michelle really is lying. I'll just have to start spending more time with her. We'll have some real mother-daughter time. Then she won't feel so threatened by Reggie.

Cassey moved to stand in his path.

"What you doing?" Reggie asked.

She took the clothes from him and took them back to the closet.

"You sure 'bout this?"

Cassey didn't respond. She continued to put his clothes back into their proper places.

Smiling, Reggie pulled her into his arms. "Now that's what I'm talking about." His mouth covered hers.

For the first time, Cassey felt no passion for him. The faint smell of alcohol, coffee and peppermint on his breath made her nauseous. She couldn't even summon her body to respond to his kiss.

He held on to her for what seemed like eternity.

In Reggie's arms, Cassey eyed the knife lying on the nightstand.

The next day, she was relieved when Reggie left to go wherever he was going. She'd had a sleepless night, tormented by images of him and Michelle. Cassey was still unable to come up with a suitable way of dealing with her daughter. Something must have happened because of all the blood.

She kept telling herself it was simply Michelle entering a new phase. She'd gotten her cycle and just got scared. Or she been messing around with Todd and got more than she bargained for.

Cassey considered threatening to take Michelle to the doctor to get the truth, but each time she reached for the phone, her courage failed. She wasn't sure she could handle the truth herself.

Reggie said he didn't do nothing and she believed him. Cassey pushed away all nagging doubts. She would ask Twana to let Michelle stay with her for a few more days until everything settled down. It would give her and Reggie some time alone and to discuss how to handle Michelle.

Knowing she couldn't put it off any longer, Cassey called Twana. "Hey. I wanted to check on Michelle."

"Really?" Twana's tone was cold. "Why, I never would've guessed."

Already feeling defensive, Cassey's mood veered sharply to anger. "Twana, don't start . . ."

"I think you saying that to the wrong person," Twana responded in the same cool tone.

"I didn't call to argue with you. Now I don't know what Michelle told you but—"

Twana cut her off. "Michelle didn't have to tell me anything. I could see it in her eyes. I could see that the poor child was in agony. Now I hope you kicked that sick—"

Cassey interrupted her. "Reggie didn't do nothing, Twana."

"Then who did?"

"She either got her cycle or she been messing 'round with that lil' niggah up the street. She always prancing her behind in his face. I had to get on her a couple of times 'bout the way she be acting 'round him."

Her comment was met with silence.

"Twana," Cassey prompted. "You there?"

"Yeah, I'm still here, but I need to get off this phone. I'ma go check on Michelle, so I'll give you a call later. She can stay with me as long as she want to."

"Wait a minute, Twana. Let me speak to Michelle."

"She's sleeping, Cassey. You can call her back later. I got to go."

"Twana, don't you hang up this phone on me."

Agitated, Cassey paced back and forth in her living room. "We been friends too long for you to treat me like this."

"I ain't treatin' you no kinda way," Twana snapped. "You doing this to yourself and yo' daughter. Michelle ain't said a word, but I believe deep down in my heart that whatever happened to her ain't got nothin' to do with Todd Barker. Reggie with his evil self is at the root of this situation. I believe that, Cassey. I can't believe you're so blind you can't see it. I seen the way that ol' snake be eyeing Michelle. He even be looking me all over."

"Twana, the man got eyes. What he s'posed to do? Walk 'round with blinders on? That's what men do—they look. I'd be worried if he were looking at men."

"Cassey, I done told you before—Reggie ain't no good man. I can't tell you not to see him. If he's who you want, then have at him, but you don't need to have him living with you and Michelle. You can't bring every man 'round yo' daughter like that."

"Reggie and I been talkin' 'bout getting married. When we do that, what I'm supposed to do with Michelle?"

"He got to get a divorce first," Twana shot back.

"Excuse me for trying to keep my family together, Twana." She stopped and took a deep breath. "Did I put Reggie over my child?" Cassey shook her head. "No. Did I put my child over Reggie? No. Did I put Cassey over both of them? You bet I did! Any woman my age knows how hard it is to keep a man. And with a child, too. Look at me, Twana. Who else am I gonna be able to get?"

"You can survive without a man, Cassey. If you wanna know the truth, sex is overrated."

"Sex might be overrated but solitude sure ain't," Cassey argued. "No matter how hard you squeeze a pillow, it don't ever squeeze back."

"You make it sound as if you the only person who ever had to go it alone," Twana interjected. "I agree it ain't easy, but it sure is doable. There are single parents raising children all over."

"Yeah . . . it's real easy for you to say. You ain't never had no children. Soon as you got pregnant, you hightailed it to one of those abortion clinics."

"You don't have to throw my business up in my face, Cassey. I know all too well what I done. I'll be the first to admit I was young and stupid back then. And believe me when I tell you that I'm payin' for it now. I can't have no children, but if I did—I sho' wouldn't be puttin' no man ahead of 'em."

"You know, it's real easy for people on the outside lookin' in to criticize. Tellin' me what I should do."

"Do you love Michelle? You got to know somethin' happened to your little girl—why you ain't here for her?"

"I love my baby. Twana, things are different today. Nowadays, they call discipline child abuse. When things go too far on a date—they call it rape."

Cassey paused a moment before saying, "When I was a kid, we were taught to just move on. Things happen, but if it don't kill you—you'll get through it." Her voice trembled as she spoke. "When it happened to me, my mama said, 'Cassey . . . don't go hatin' yo daddy . . . we all got our cross to bear. . . .'"

"If you ain't gon' be here for her—I am. I gotta go. Michelle needs me."

Twana hung up.

9

Bishop Jakes studied Michelle, noticing how small she looked, a child in a woman's body, really.

"You think that what happened that day set your life on this path?"

"Just like the domino theory," Michelle answered with quiet emphasis. "With the way my life went, crap was destined to wind up on my plate."

"Isn't that why we wash dishes?"

"Easier said than done, Bishop," she countered thickly.

"It's never too late, Michelle."

Her eyes darkened with pain and she couldn't seem to be able to lift her voice above a whisper. "It is for me." Michelle fought back unshed tears.

She admired her handywork. "I think this is probably my best work," she murmured.

Bishop Jakes said what Michelle knew he would: "It's not too late for you."

Giving him a sidelong glance, she uttered, "I appreciate you saying that, Bishop. You do your job well."

"I want to help you, Michelle."

Michelle studied his face in the dim lighting of the cell. After a moment she nodded. "I believe you do. There was a time I actually thought that was possible, but now . . ." She shook her head. "Not anymore. Sad thing is, even if it was, I don't think I deserve it."

It didn't take Todd much effort to talk Michelle into having a late dinner with him after the service on Friday night. He took her to a restaurant four blocks away from the cathedral.

Seated in a booth, they made small talk while waiting on their food. Michelle dove in as soon as their meals arrived.

Todd regarded her with amusement. "You trying to finish that up before it spoils?"

"Hmmm?"

It took a moment for Michelle to realize that she'd been wolfing down her food. Twana was always on her case about being more ladylike.

"Go on, eat. It was just a little gluttony humor."

"Very little," she stated dryly. "I'm sure you crack your wife up all the time."

"I don't have a wife."

Michelle stopped eating long enough to say, "I thought you said you were married to Keisha."

"I'm married," Todd admitted. "But I don't have a wife. About a year ago I pulled my credit report. Found a loan for a Hummer that I didn't buy. Turns out she met some baggy-pants snot-nose thug—he couldn't have been more than nineteen—that was taking her for a ride."

"Literally."

"Yeah, I guess so. By the time I found out, they were long gone and I was broke, deep in debt and a single parent. The only thing they hadn't gotten to was the house I bought my mother."

"That's messed up. He must have been puttin' something on her that you weren't."

"Thanks. You always knew just what to say."

Michelle shrugged. "Hey, I been in prison. That's what we think about."

"That place must have been something else."

"Jail?"

The two women seated in the booth ahead of them glanced over. When they found Michelle watching them, they quickly turned away.

"You hear all those wild stories but you know the saying: believe half of what you see, none of what you hear."

She took a long sip of water, looking at Todd look at her.

Putting the glass down, Michelle asked, "What? You want a story? You want to hear about some of the stuff I went through in there? Okay. I'll entertain you. First, there's the prison guard whose jugular I cut from here to here . . . ," she said, moving her finger from one side of her neck to the other.

Michelle hid her amusement when the women shooed away their waitress in order to eavesdrop without interruption. She decided to give them and Todd exactly what they wanted to hear.

"Then there's the time I escaped and hid in a sewage tank for three days before they caught up with me. . . ."

"That's too bad."

"Oh, wait . . . I bet the freak in you would rather hear about the hos who tried to rape me my first day there. Typical shower scenario. I'm minding my own business and somebody sneaks up from behind and puts me in a choke hold. Another girl pulls my hair. The third pulls my legs . . ." She paused a moment before adding, "Same way I'm pulling yours right now."

Michelle threw her head back laughing.

"What? You made all that up?"

She nodded. "None of that stuff happened . . . except the shower thing. . . ." Leaning forward, she said to the old woman eavesdropping from the other booth, "You were there, weren't you?"

Todd gave her a sheepish grin. "I guess I had that coming."

"*You guess?*" Michelle sat back against the cushions of the booth. "I didn't have nothing really happen to me. I just did my time—minded my own business." In a louder voice, she added, "Like some folks can't seem to do."

A tall man entered the restaurant and Michelle's expression suddenly changed. "Oh no . . ."

"What is it?" Todd glanced over his shoulder. "Who's that? Old boyfriend?"

"Worse. That's Eli. Your friendly neighborhood dope man."

She dropped her eyes as he neared their table.

When his steps slowed, she muttered a curse.

"Hey yo . . . Michelle."

She turned away, pretending not to know him.

It soon became apparent that Eli wasn't going to just leave.

"Remember me? It's Eli. . . . Now I know you not gon' play dumb, as much as I used to tighten you up. I didn't know you got out."

Michelle's gaze met Todd's briefly before turning to the drug dealer.

"Yeah, Eli. I remember you."

She pushed the food around on her plate, wishing Eli would just disappear. He reminded her of everything she wanted to forget.

Ignoring Todd completely, Eli slid into the seat beside her. "Look here. I ain't gettin' chicks wet for Pervis no more. Brotha is moving on up. Same rules apply though."

He checked out the restaurant before adding in a low voice, "The first one is on me. What you need?"

Michelle shook her head vehemently. "I don't get wet no more."

Stroking the fine hair on his chin, Eli chuckled. "That's what they all say, sweetheart."

Her gaze meeting Todd's, Michelle responded, "Well, I'm really flyin' straight this time."

"That's good to hear." Eli's eyes swept around the restaurant before continuing. "I never approved of what Pervis was doin' to y'all, but I'm a businessman, too. Know what I'm saying? I mean . . . my kids want Big Wheels and PlayStations just like everybody else's."

"Legit is always an option."

He shook his head. "But not for me. I can't make this kind of money in a legitimate job. My family . . . we gotta lifestyle we want to maintain. Know what I'm saying? I'm just trying to take care of my family. I'm a family man."

Eli reached into his pocket and pulled out a bag of crack, which he set down in front of Michelle. "From me to you. You don't want it—flush it."

Todd cleared his throat noisily, catching Eli's attention. Eli squinted at him. "Hey, bro, don't I know you?"

"Officer Barker, Narcotics division," Todd stated. He held out his hand to Eli. "Nice to meet you."

Michelle bit back her smile. She'd always loved Todd's subtle wit.

Eli glanced over at Michelle, then back at Todd. "You . . . you for real, yo?"

Dropping his hand, Todd inquired, "You got ID on you?"

"Naw . . . naw. I was at a pool party." Eli rushed to his feet, saying, "I gotta go. Michelle . . . good seeing ya. I'll holla at ya later."

Todd began, "Don't forget your—"

Eli cut him off by saying, "That ain't mine."

He practically ran over a couple in his attempt to leave the restaurant in a hurry.

Michelle and Todd shared a laugh.

"Not bad," she admitted. "I had my doubts, but you might just be able to make it on the inside after all."

Todd grinned. "I'll take that as a compliment." He paused a moment, then looked deeply into Michelle's eyes. "I just want you to know that it doesn't make any difference to me."

Michelle eyed him with a calculating expression. "What doesn't?"

"You know—the record, drugs . . . none of it."

Todd's comment irked her.

Folding her arms across her chest, she leaned back against the booth. "Wow . . . you mean to tell me squeaky clean, geeky church boy Todd Barker is willing to overlook my flaws? *I am truly lucky.*"

The expression on Todd's face changed. "That's not what I meant, Michelle."

"I don't care what you meant by it."

After a moment of tense silence, Todd suggested, "Look, maybe I'd better take you home."

"Yeah, maybe you'd better."

Michelle pushed her plate away and slipped out of the booth while Todd signaled for the check.

"I'll be outside," she mumbled. *He got some nerve—like he so perfect. I don't need him or anybody else.*

Todd was flabbergasted by the sudden turn of events.

How could things have taken such a quick turn for the worse? All he was trying to do was express his feelings for Michelle.

He stole a peek over his shoulder to see if she was still standing outside the restaurant.

She was.

Relieved, Todd hurried to pay the check before Michelle just took off and left.

Just like when they were kids, she would only let him get so close—then this wall would come shooting up.

How do I make you understand how much I care about you? he asked in silence. There were so many times he wanted to say those words to Michelle, but Todd knew to do so would send her running away so fast. He wasn't ready to risk it.

For now, he had to play by Michelle's rules.

Todd parked his car in front of the halfway house and turned off the ignition. All the lights were off in the house.

"It's late. You sure you can get in?" he inquired.

Nodding, Michelle answered, "Yeah. I asked Nicole to wait up for me. Just in case I didn't make it back in time for curfew."

He reached over and took her by the hand. "Listen . . . I didn't mean . . ."

Michelle gently removed her hand from his. "No apology necessary. All right?"

Todd nodded. "Can I pick you up tomorrow?"

She thought it over for a moment, then shook her head no. "I'd rather not make a habit of this."

"Of what?"

Michelle stared straight ahead. "This . . . you and me."

"So, what are you saying?"

"How about if we just holla at each other now and then?" she suggested. Michelle didn't see any point in prolonging the inevitable.

"Look at you, Michelle." Todd was staring at her in amazement.

"Why you looking at me like that?"

"It's just that . . ." His voice died. He shook his head and continued, "You used to be so fearless—so smart. I just don't see how somebody like you could . . ."

"Could go so wrong, huh?" Michelle finished his statement for him.

Todd shook his head in denial. "Not necessarily wrong," he clarified for her, "just sidetracked."

Michelle kept her gaze straight ahead. "When you're hanging by a rope with nowhere to climb, a fall is inevitable. Eventually you get tired, so why not just let go?"

"You had everything. I mean everybody in the neighborhood was so envious of the Jordans. We were on welfare—your family wasn't. We were living in this raggedy apartment and you were living in a real house."

She shot him a withering glance. "Lucky me, huh?"

"Look, Michelle . . . I know you never liked to talk about what went on in your home. But you had a mother and a stepfather who loved you."

"He's not my stepfather, Todd. He ain't nothin' to me," she quickly interjected.

"I didn't have any kind of father. Step or otherwise. Isn't a bad one better than none at all? You know how tough it was to grow up without a father? I mean, my moms tried, but I never had any kind of male role model in my life. No one to teach me how to be a man."

"I think you turned out okay."

"It wasn't easy. Then when you left me, I was devastated—"

Michelle cut him off. "Todd, that wasn't about you."

"I know that now, but back then I didn't know what to think. I didn't know anything at all, except that I hurt inside."

Michelle shifted uncomfortably, not sure where this was going.

"After Keisha left me, I just about lost it. This time, I wasn't so much hurt as I was angry. There was a rage inside of me, ready to explode. I even started drinking too much, using alcohol to escape those feelings I didn't know how to handle.

"But then I remembered my daughter. I know what it was like to not have a father. I didn't want the same for her. So I got help."

"Help?"

"I started seeing a therapist, Michelle."

"You went to a shrink?"

Todd looked at her, unashamed. "It was the smartest thing I ever did. My daughter's mother ran away. She didn't need her father to run away, too."

Michelle didn't know how to respond, so she said nothing and looked away.

"You know," Todd said, "sometimes just talking to someone about things can make a world of difference. I wish you would've talked to me back then, before you ran away."

Michelle had shared her body with Todd but could never share what had transpired between her and Reggie all those years. She supposed she didn't want him to think any less of her at the time. Even now she still couldn't tell him.

"Gotta get some shut-eye. Good-bye, Todd. . . ."

After a moment, he replied, "Every good-bye ain't gone."

Michelle glanced over at him. "Huh?"

"They say . . . Every good-bye ain't gone. Every shut-eye ain't sleep, and every house ain't home. It just hit me. . . ." Todd paused for a moment. "Your house never was home, was it? What happened in there?"

Michelle stepped out of the car. Leaning down, she responded, "You know what else they say? If you don't like the song they're playin', hum something else."

She sauntered away humming a jazzy tune.

Michelle stole a glance across her shoulder.

Todd was sitting there with his mouth hanging open just like he used to do when they were kids.

Striking a pretty pose, she waved, saying, "Good night, Todd."

10

"I really don't remember crying another tear after the night Reggie stole my innocence. I think I know now that little girls like me don't really grow up. They just die." Michelle paused as she applied a matchstick to the tiny house. "I stayed almost two weeks over at Twana's house. When I went back home, it wasn't the same ever again. I wasn't the same."

"They don't always die, Michelle," Bishop Jakes countered. "Sometimes they just go into hiding. It's the only way they can protect themselves from the world."

She gave him a deadly look. "And the world better protect itself from me."

"The worst harm you'll ever do is to yourself."

Michelle chuckled. "I know a DA and a judge that might disagree with you."

"Even they would find it strange that neither you nor your mother uttered a word about the molestations during your trial."

"My mother is a piece of work. She swears she ain't got no memory of anything. And you know what? I halfway believe her. She's always had this 'don't look—don't tell' policy. And if she's convinced wasn't nothing ill going on between her daughter and her man—then nothing happened as far as she was concerned. She just kept on looking the other way."

Michelle pointed to her work in progress. "Window or no window, Bishop?"

"Window."

"I knew you'd say that. Let me guess. A window symbolizes opportunity. To see out, to gain access, or just to catch a breath of fresh air. . . . Am I right?"

Bishop Jakes's dark eyes pierced the distance between them. "The warden has personally petitioned the governor for a temporary stay. Your attorney seems to think that you won't have much trouble getting a new trial."

"I won't hold my breath, Bishop."

The guard returned, pressing his face to the bars.

"It's mealtime, Bishop," he announced. "If she eats, you'll have to step out until she's done."

"He can stay," Michelle interjected. "I'm not eating anytime soon. You hungry, Bishop?"

"No, I'm fine, but thank you."

Michelle gave the guard an amused look. "How about you, Melvin? You look like you ain't been skipping no meals."

"You know we're not allowed," he responded.

The guard left as quietly as he came.

"Why do you think Cassey would stay in such an abusive relationship for so long?"

"Now that you would have to ask her about."

"I did."

"You know the story about the man walking down a country road and notices his neighbor's dog on the front porch?"

Bishop Jakes shook his head. "No, I don't. Why don't you tell me."

"The dog is squirmin', and moanin' and groanin' so much that this man goes and asks his neighbor, 'What's wrong?' The neighbor says, 'Nothin' . . . my dog's just lyin' on a nail.' So he says, 'Why don't he just get movin'?' And the neighbor says, 'I don't know . . . I guess he ain't hurtin' bad enough yet.'"

Michelle stopped to admire her work—a matchstick porch.

Holding it up for him to see, she asked, "Know what a porch is for, Bishop? It's a segue. You're not quite inside yet. And you ain't all the way outside."

"Is that where you are?" Bishop Jakes questioned.

Nodding, Michelle answered, "I've been on the porch ever since I left home."

Michelle stood on the front lawn, staring at her home as if seeing it for the first time. The white house with the black trim no longer felt like home to her. She had hoped her mother would've agreed to let her live with Twana.

Cassey walked out on the porch, her hands on her hips. "Well, you just gon' stand out there all day long? Child, you better bring yo' lil' rusty behind on in this house."

Twana took her by the hand. "C'mon, Michelle."

She was fine until Reggie joined her mother on the porch.

He wrapped an arm around Cassey and said, "Well . . . it's 'bout time you came back home, Michelle."

Just hearing his voice made Michelle's skin crawl. She eyed Cassey in disbelief.

Twana knelt down in front of her, whispering, "Honey, if you want to come back over to my house, just let me know. I'll come get you right away."

"Home's where she belong," Reggie stated. "Cassey and I are her parents. So you just mind yo' business."

"You ain't nothing to her," Twana responded.

"Y'all don't start . . . ," Cassey warned. "Thanks for bringing Michelle home, Twana. But it's time for you to leave. We need to have a family discussion."

"Humph," Twana grunted.

"You heard Cassey," Reggie interjected. "Leave."

"You can't tell me nothing." Twana pulled up her tube top while she talked. "I don't know who you think you are, but you don't scare me." She took a step toward him.

Cassey inserted her body between them. "Twana, you go on home. I'll give you a call later."

When her godmother headed back to her car, Michelle ached to leave with her. She didn't want to stay in this house as long as Reggie was living there.

Cassey gave Michelle a tiny push. "Let's go inside, Michelle. We need to have a lil' talk."

Reggie held the door open for her.

She looked back at Cassey, who sighed in exasperation.

"Child, get yo' behind in the house. Whacha waitin' on? Christmas?"

Michelle's eyes met Reggie's gaze briefly.

He winked at her.

She shuddered as a deep sense of dread spread through her body.

A few minutes later, the three of them were seated in the living room.

Michelle sat with her hands folded in her lap, her eyes staring down at the floor.

"I feel like I need to make some things clear to you, Michelle. Now I don't appreciate the way you treated your Uncle Reggie. He—"

Michelle cut her off by saying, "He's not my uncle."

Reggie laughed.

Cassey sent a sharp look his way, silencing him. "I'm not gon' tolerate any disrespect."

Michelle stood up. "Can I go to my room? I don't feel good."

"I'm not through talkin' to yo—"

This time Reggie interrupted her. "Let her go, Cassey. Sooner or later, she gon' get with the program. Ain't you, Michelle? You can make it easy for yo'self or you can make it hard. It's yo' choice."

His eyes issued a silent challenge.

Michelle swept past them without a response.

That night she put a chair against her locked door to keep Reggie out.

With Michelle back in the house, Cassey didn't sleep well. She kept waking up at every little sound.

When Reggie crept out of bed, she pretended to be asleep. He strode out of the room and she eased out of bed, tiptoeing to see where he was going. She leaned against the door in relief when he walked into the bathroom.

She ran back to the bed and closed her eyes when she heard him flushing the toilet.

Reggie came into the bedroom and climbed back into bed. Within minutes he'd fallen back to sleep.

Cassey felt terrible over doubting him, but there were still thoughts in the back of her mind that just would not go away— no matter how hard she tried to escape them. She considered asking Reggie to move out for a few days, but didn't really know if he'd come back. She wasn't willing to risk losing him, despite the fact that she didn't really trust him. She'd just be watching his every move whenever Michelle was around.

The two weren't speaking to each other, although she had noticed that Reggie initially tried to go out of his way to be nice to Michelle.

Reggie turned on his side and pulled her body to his. Cassey smiled as she felt him snuggling closer. She loved him. They would get through this together.

But in the meantime, Cassey decided that she would keep

Michelle away from home whenever Reggie was going to be there.

Reggie came home with a huge teddy bear and some roses.

Michelle was at the living room table doing her homework and Cassey was in the kitchen cooking.

As soon as he walked in, Michelle rose to her feet and began packing up her books. "I'm gon' finish my homework in my room," she announced.

He blocked her path. "Hey, Michelle. You ain't got to leave. I brought something for you."

She glared at him.

Cassey joined them. "That's a nice bear. He's a real beauty, don't you think, Michelle? You love teddy bears."

Michelle didn't say anything.

"Well, you gon' take it?" he snapped impatiently. "I didn't have to go out and spend all this money on this bear for you. I wanted to do something nice for my family and this is the appreciation I get?"

Reggie turned to Cassey. "Here, baby. These for you."

Cassey took the flowers and smelled them. "Thank you, honey." She gave him a kiss fully on the lips.

"Now see, Michelle," Reggie gloated. "That's how you supposed to act. You should be appreciative. Now give me a kiss on the cheek."

"I don't want the bear," she stated.

Cassey gasped. "Michelle, what's got into you?"

She didn't respond.

When Michelle walked off to her bedroom, Reggie itched to follow her. He wanted to slap some sense into her.

He was going out of his way to make peace with her and she thwarted his every attempt. Michelle wouldn't say more than a few words to him at a time and she made sure she was never left alone in a room with him.

Reggie knew Cassey was watching him, too. At times, it made him angry, but he maintained his composure. He would simply bide his time.

Michelle wasn't going anywhere.

Delores knocked on the door announcing, "Jordan, you got a guest outside on the porch."

Michelle checked herself in the mirror, running her fingers through her spiral curls. Satisfied, she grabbed her jacket, complaining, "Todd, what you doin' here now?"

She threw open her door and rushed out, bumping into Delores, the director of the house.

"Slow down, Jordan. He's not going anywhere."

Michelle rolled her eyes at the woman, but slowed her pace.

When she stepped out on the porch, Michelle glanced around in confusion.

She didn't see Todd's car anywhere on the street. If he wasn't her visitor then who?

Michelle felt the hair on the back of her neck stand up.

Before she could react, someone grabbed her from behind, startling her.

"*Hey,*" Michelle shouted and wrenched her body away from

her captor. With her hands balled into fists, Michelle spun around to face her attacker.

"I heard you were back home."

Some of Michelle's tension evaporated, but she still kept her guard up. "Pervis, I was wondering how long it would be before you showed up."

"Just because you paid your debt to society don't mean you paid your debt to me." He reached out to finger an errant spiral curl.

"But I will," Michelle promised as she took a step back. "I ain't even got a job yet and you sweatin' me."

"Yeah ya do . . . ," Pervis countered. "Your old job is still waiting for you at the club. Best hooker I ever had."

"I might not look like it on the outside, but that ain't me no more. I'm even going to church. I'm just trying to keep my sanity."

"Unless you got my five thousand dollars on you right now, you'll be butt naked and swinging around a pole tonight."

"You can't get blood from a turnip."

Click.

Michelle's eyes strayed down to the knife that was now pressed against her arm.

"But I can from a crackhead."

Calm and unshaken, Michelle raised her chin in defiance. "What? You gonna kill me over some money?"

"I might. . . . I should. . . ."

"Right out in the open like this? You really are dumber than you look."

"Look at you. The Michelle I used to know would be crying like a baby right now. What they do to you in prison?"

"Nothing compared to what they did to me out here."

"You ain't seen nothing if you don't get my money." Pervis cut into her arm, drawing blood.

"You might wanna aim for my wrists if you really wanna take me out."

"Oh, you think you hard now?" Pervis slapped her. "I'll show you hard."

Michelle slapped him back. "Is this how they been treating women since I've been gone?"

Enraged, Pervis reached for her throat. "You crazy? Girl, I'll kill you. . . ." He punched Michelle as hard as he could. "You wanna act like a man, I'll beat you down like a man."

She fell to the ground in a heap.

Pervis continued beating on her. "You gonna be at my club tonight. You hear me?"

Images of her and Nicole smoking a crack pipe materialized in Michelle's mind.

"You think you ever gonna find another man like me?" He delivered another blow.

A vision of her in bed with Pervis . . .

"As good as I been to you," he shouted and hit her again.

Michelle could see herself dancing around a pole as a bunch of perverted patrons stretched and threw dollar bills in her direction.

Another blow. "You think you can do any better than me?"

Another memory invaded her thoughts. The one with Michelle resisting Pervis's advances. She could vividly recall the brutal beating and the sexual assault that followed.

"Don't nobody want your sorry behind but me."

Michelle fended off as many of Pervis's blows as she could. Pain raged through her body and she felt herself getting weaker, but she wouldn't give up. He would have to kill her before she'd go back to stripping.

"Oww . . ."

Pervis fell forward, face-first.

Stunned, Michelle glanced up and found Nicole standing over them holding a bloodied two-by-four.

"That's for taking my family," she shouted.

Pervis lay on the porch writhing in pain.

Nicole assisted Michelle up. "C'mon, let's get out of here."

Michelle kicked Pervis as hard as she could manage without falling back down. Leaning on Nicole, she limped back into the house.

They met the director coming down the stairs as they were headed up.

Delores gasped. "What in the world? . . ."

"Ain't nothin' to worry 'bout," Michelle managed through bleeding lips. "I just fell down the steps."

"You fell? That don't look like—"

Nicole held up a hand to interrupt Delores. "She said she fell. *All right?*"

Michelle winced as she walked gingerly up a flight of stairs. Her body throbbed with pain all over.

In their bedroom, Nicole inquired, "You gon' be able to make it to church tonight?"

"I gotta go."

Examining her face, Nicole frowned. "That's ugly."

"Thanks."

Delores walked into their room without knocking. "Here, put this on your eye."

Michelle took the wet cloth and placed it to her face. The coldness provided temporary relief.

Shaking her head, Delores twisted her mouth into a frown. "Humph. That sho' don't look like a fall. Unless you fell on somebody's fist."

"Thank you for the rag, Delores." Michelle waved her hand in dismissal. "I got it from here."

When the director left the room, Nicole asked, "You think Pervis still on the porch?"

"If he wanna live—he better be gone." Michelle groaned in pain when she tried to sit down. "This the last time he gon' beat me down like this."

"I know that's right," Nicole agreed. "Ain't nobody going out like that. Not no more."

Michelle and Nicole sat in silence for a moment.

Nicole broke the silence. "Hey, is it okay if I take you up on that church offer?"

"Sure." Michelle lay down on her bed. "I'm gonna rest for a while." She hoped the pain would be gone by the time she had to leave for church.

"Twana, you seen Michelle?" Cassey inquired as she walked into the salon. "I been lookin' around for her."

"Not today, but she supposed to be coming to revival tonight . . . and I think she's coming with Todd Barker."

"Todd? What she doin' with him?" Cassey met her gaze. "Don't that girl know how to stay away from trouble?"

"Lay off him, Cassey. He's a good guy and I heard Michelle and Todd been hangin' tough." Twana broke into a short laugh. "She might be givin' him some."

Shaking her head, Cassey uttered, "You need Jesus."

"What? The girl been locked up in prison."

Rolling her eyes heavenward, Cassey said, "If you do see her—tell her she can meet the bishop after service."

"Girl, you do have clout."

Laughing, Twana and Cassey high-fived.

"I been working at that church long enough. I really been praying for her and Reggie to get saved."

"Humph. What needs to be saved is your relationship with your daughter."

Cassey placed her hands on ample hips. "Twana, don't you think I been trying? I got her out of that place early. I got Bishop to talk to her."

"Have *you* talked to her?"

"We talked a little while yesterday before Reggie came to pick me up."

Twana looked at her in surprise. "Locked up all this time and that's the best you can do? Give her five minutes?"

Lifting her chin, Cassey met Twana's gaze straight on. "Look, that girl cursed me out to my face before she went to jail." Lowering her voice, she added, "Reggie don't want her back in that house."

"*Reggie?* You still puttin' that man before your own flesh and blood?"

"There's a lot you don't know."

Twana nodded. "True that. I don't know what went on in that house behind closed doors. But I sho' got my suspicions."

"Twana, don't start. . . . now come on and help me with my hair. Reggie gonna pick me up soon and take me grocery shopping before I head over to revival." Cassey gave her a gentle push.

Twana shook her head in resignation and muttered under her breath, "Shoot, it ain't yo' hair, girl. It's yo' head that needs some fixin'."

Cassey struggled to get the bag of groceries out of the trunk of the car. She shifted them to her strong side and made her way up the steps and into the house. Reggie got out, slamming the door, and rushed after her.

"Cassey, hold on. . . ."

Irritated, she paused in her steps. "Whacha want?"

Instead of giving her any assistance with the groceries, Reggie reached inside the heavy bag she was holding and removed a six-pack of beer. "You smashing my doggone beer!"

Without preamble, he opened one, put the others back in the bag and took a seat.

Disgusted, Cassey stood there glaring at him.

After a moment, Reggie glanced her way. "What, you want a sip?"

"A little help would be nice." Cassey set the bag on the kitchen counter and began emptying out the contents.

Reggie's eyes darkened as he held her gaze. "I'm head of this household. If that ain't help enough, I can't do no more."

She could only stare at him. His comment had left her momentarily speechless. When she found her voice, Cassey uttered, "Head of the household? Judging by your W-2s, *dependent* might be more like it."

Reggie's mouth took on an unpleasant twist. "Used to be a day when you said something like that, I'd slap you silly."

Turning around, Cassey leaned against the counter with her arms folded across her chest. "Those days are long gone, Reggie. And never to come back again." She shook her head in dismay. "I don't know what I was thinking back then."

The room was bathed in tense silence.

Turning away from Reggie, Cassey resumed her task of putting away the groceries.

He slapped her on her behind as she walked by him to get to the refrigerator. "Now, I just keep you in check with some good lovin'."

"And there ain't gonna be no more of that either, Reggie," Cassey warned. "I can't keep living in sin."

"Here we go again. . . ." He sighed. "How much longer do I need to put up with this revival?"

"Two more days."

"*Two more days?* Ain't nothin' in this house to eat. What I'm s'posed to do?"

"Your dinner for tonight and tomorrow are in the freezer, Reggie. All you need to do is put them in the microwave. Don't forget to take the lid off. You know, you might want to drop in one of those nights and give your life to the Lord."

"I'm already going to heaven." Reggie's expression was taut and derisive. "It's you and those hypocrites at that church that need to be worried 'bout gettin' in."

"At least I'm trying to live right."

"Loving me is living right," Reggie insisted with impatience. "I don't care what they telling you at that church."

"Reggie, we been living in sin for more than fifteen years," Cassey exclaimed in irritation. "I'm tired of trying to hide the truth that we live together and wearing this ring that don't mean nothin'. This just ain't right."

"Whacha want me to do? You know my divorce ain't final. That woman never did sign the paperwork."

"That woman's moved on with her life," Cassey argued. "She's got three kids by her new boyfriend. I'm not stupid. I know what you doing, Reggie. You thinking that if she dies, you gonna get something if you stay married to her."

"And what's wrong with that?"

Cassey sighed in resignation. "I don't blame you—I blame me. All I know is I can't do this anymore. If you don't change something soon, and I mean this weekend, you got to move out."

"Move out? Where?"

She pointed toward the front door. "Out there. Somewhere. Anywhere."

Reggie got up and walked over to Cassey, giving her a brutal stare. "Oh, it's like that? After all these years, you and God just gon' gangsta me like that."

"Nobody can force you to do anything. This is more about me than about you," Cassey explained. "We need God to forgive us."

Reaching for her, he pulled Cassey into his arms. "People do the best they can, baby. We did the best we could. Ain't no need in being ashamed of that."

Her heart said what her mouth could not whenever Reggie was this close to her. *What we doing is wrong.*

11

"How many of you know that nothing just happens?"

Bishop Jakes had just begun his sermon for the evening. "Three women—Naomi, who was the older woman, and Ruth, who was her daughter-in-law, and Orpah, who was her other daughter-in-law—three women whose commonality was pain. Pain is a strange company keeper. It brings the oddest people together. There is a secret fraternity that exists amongst those who have been in pain that is mind-boggling. It transcends the color of your skin. It transcends your background. When you have been through certain things, you feel for other people who have been through those things, because you relate to them."

Michelle listened to the preacher's words as she and Nicole

stood in the foyer of the cathedral. It had taken her a while to get to revival because her body was sore and her head aching.

Hearing Bishop Jakes now caused Michelle to pause and consider his words.

She couldn't help but notice that people stared at her as they walked by. Self-conscious, she turned to Nicole, asking, "How do I look?"

"Like you pissed off Lennox Lewis."

Feeling defensive, Michelle put a hand to her face and responded, "It really don't matter how I look anyway. It ain't a fashion show."

Nicole glanced over at two young women dressed in tailored suits with matching hat and accessories who strutted past them.

She gave Michelle a soft jab. "Oh yes it is. Did you see what they were wearing?"

"Shut up, girl," she whispered. "Go on inside and get us a seat, I'll be right back."

Biting her lower lip, Michelle strolled over to a nearby usher. "Have you seen Cassey Jordan? I'm her daughter."

The woman pointed toward the prayer room.

Cassey was on her knees with her eyes closed when Michelle entered.

Michelle cleared her throat noisily, but her mother didn't seem to notice. She was busy praying.

For what? she wondered.

Michelle stood there for a while silently watching her.

No prayer can be that long, she thought. Michelle finally decided to interrupt. "Cassey?"

Hearing her name, Cassey turned around, her eyes full of tears.

Cassey's expression turned to concern when she saw the bruises on her daughter's face. "Michelle? What?. . . What happened to your face?"

She rose, walking over to her daughter, reaching out a hand to touch her face.

Backing away, Michelle responded, "I don't want to discuss that right now."

· "But you need some ice or something, baby."

"Just let it be, Cassey." Michelle paused. "The usher told me I could find you in here."

"I was praying for someone."

"I kicked that habit a long time ago." Michelle leaned forward and whispered, "Here's a little-known secret. Prayer don't work."

"It got you here."

Michelle broke into a bitter laugh. "And here I was giving Greyhound all the credit. Silly me."

"Baby, I'm sorry about that. I don't know what to do," Cassey confessed. "It's Reggie. He didn't want you at the house. What was I gonna do? Pick you up and take you where?"

Michelle swallowed hard, lifted her chin and met her mother's gaze. "How about taking me in your arms, Cassey? That would've been a first."

Cassey took a deep breath. Her voice filled with resignation, she stated, "Michelle, I know I haven't done everything just right. . . ."

"You let a man molest your own daughter."

"Keep your voice down, Michelle."

Michelle's eyes narrowed and hardened. "Still don't want anybody to know?"

"Michelle, pleeze," Cassey snapped in anger. "Don't start with those old lies again in the house of God."

"How can this be the house of God when hypocrites like you hang out here?"

Cassey stiffened. "Excuse me?"

Michelle snatched up Cassey's left hand. Pointing to the narrow gold wedding band, she stated, "You and Reggie. Y'all ain't married, but I bet you got this whole church believing otherwise."

"You shut yo' mouth," Cassey ordered as she snatched her hand away. "What goes on in my house is my business."

"Are you sure *you* know what's going on in your house, 'cause you act like you don't. Reggie's not the saint you want to pretend he is."

"I never said he was a saint," Cassey countered. "But Michelle, you got no room to talk—all the things you done. You tried to kill Reggie."

"He was trying to rape me." Michelle's voice grew an octave higher. "You don't want to accept the truth, but that's the real deal. Your man has been molesting me for years, and then he tried to rape me one night at the strip club."

"Reggie said he was tryin' to get you to come home," Cassey sputtered with indignation.

Michelle's laughter was harsh. "And you actually believe that? That pervert sat in the club and watched me take my clothes off. He even stuck money in my G-string—he tell you that?"

Cassey tried to walk away, but Michelle stood in her way.

"Did he?" she asked.

"This discussion is over. I need to get to work and you need to be in the sanctuary listening to Bishop Jakes. You got too much hatred in your heart, Michelle. You need to find a way to get past all your anger. It's only gonna bring you nothing but more grief."

"I'll let go when you acknowledge the truth, Cassey. The truth that you allowed your man to rape your daughter over and over again."

"This is why Reggie don't want you at the house."

"Who's house is it?" Michelle questioned.

Without waiting for a response she stormed out of the prayer room.

Michelle walked a few steps then stopped and leaned against a wall, defeated. After all this time, her mother was still denying the truth.

How can she be blind to all the pain I went through? Michelle cried to herself. *She closed her eyes to the bruises on my body and the dying of my soul, and her eyes are still shut tight. How could she not see what was going on in that house?*

Involuntarily, Michelle's mind traveled back to the small house on Lockhart Avenue that was her hell. . . .

She could smell the alcohol on his breath as he held her thirteen-year-old body pinned down against the mattress.

For a year, Reggie hadn't bothered her . . . until now.

Cassey was at work and Michelle had been working on a book report.

But then Reggie arrived home reeking of liquor. She'd run off to her room, locking the door, but he managed to bust right inside.

This time, Michelle decided to fight back with everything she had. But Reggie soon had the better of her.

"Get off me," Michelle screamed as she continued to fight him. "I'm gon' tell my mama."

"She not gonna believe a big liar like you." Reggie gripped a handful of her hair in his hands and pulled. "Besides, if you do, I'll kill you in your sleep. You ought to stop walking around here teasing me with yo' fast behind. I know what you doing with that boy down the street. I'm the one taking care of you— you should be givin' me what you been givin' to that punk," he spat.

"Leave me alone," Michelle uttered.

"I'll leave you alone all right. When I'm done."

Michelle scrunched up her face, her eyes tightly closed shut.

"Look at me," Reggie demanded. "I bet you ain't closing yo' eyes when that boy on top of you."

Her body trembling, Michelle opened her eyes. She looked around her and saw a few older church ladies looking at her. She took a deep breath, trying to compose herself, and headed into the sanctuary to find Nikki.

Nicole had found seats toward the back and Michelle quickly made her way over to her. Her friend eyed her warily, sensing that something wasn't right.

"Girl, you okay? You look like you've seen a ghost. And you're all sweaty. Whacha do? Run a marathon?"

Michelle brushed her off. "I'm fine."

"You are not fine. Tell me what happened," Nicole implored.

When a woman in front of them turned around and glared at them, Nicole snapped, "No one's talkin' to you." Then she turned back to Michelle. "Did you find Cassey? Did she say something?"

"Oh, she said something all right, but it's nothing I haven't heard before. Same old thing. Defending Reggie and callin' me a liar right to my face."

Nicole put her hand on her friend's arm and said, "Girl, I'm sorry. I can't even imagine it. Your stepdaddy treatin' you like that all those years, and your mama not doing anything . . . still not doing anything."

Michelle didn't respond. There wasn't anything to say.

Although she tried to concentrate on Bishop Jakes's words, her mind kept straying back to those awful images of Reggie hurting her. She remembered how she didn't sleep for three days after he resumed his sexual abuse. She was afraid Reggie would creep into her room in the middle of the night. But he wasn't that dumb. He would never do anything while Cassey was home. It was during the day, when Cassey was at work, that Michelle had to worry. She dreaded the end of the school day, and would try to find things to do so she wouldn't have to go home. One of her teachers thought it so odd that Michelle would hang around after school so often that she actually called Cassey to inquire if something was going on in the house.

Boy, did Michelle hear it for that. Cassey called her a liar and threatened to beat her unconscious if she ever uttered those vicious accusations again. At that point, Michelle vowed to keep silent about her private hell.

Not even Twana could get her to unburden her soul.

Soon, her godmother simply stopped asking, even though Michelle had a feeling that Twana knew exactly what was going on between her and Reggie.

It was during that time that Michelle turned to marijuana. It was an escape. It made her feel good—or at least let her forget how bad she felt. She had slowly graduated to cocaine and other drugs. Anything to take away her pain.

Cassey got all in her face about the drugs and the trouble she'd get into. Guess she found it easier to yell at her daughter than listen to what she was trying to tell her.

Cassey found weed in a pair of Michelle's jeans.

Holding it in her hands, she laid into her daughter. "Michelle, you gon' have to find yo'self someplace else to live if you keep going the way you are. I'm not gon' have no drug addict up in my house."

Michelle rolled her eyes and looked away from her mother.

"Look at me when I'm talking to you, girl. You may be fifteen, but you ain't grown. Not in this house. And you ain't too old for me to knock you upside yo' head."

Michelle continued ignoring her.

"Don't you be bringing no weed in my house. You hear me, Michelle?"

She faced her mother then. "I hear you."

"What happened to you?" Cassey questioned. "I don't know what to do with you."

Michelle climbed off her bed. "I need to go to the bathroom."

Cassey sighed in frustration. "I'm getting real sick and tired of yo' lil' ways, Michelle. If you don't like the way we do things 'round here, then maybe you should leave. I'm not gon' have you disrespecting me. You hear me?"

"I hear you, Cassey. I hear you. Now can I pleeze go to the bathroom?"

Cassey had to resist the urge to wrap her fingers around her daughter's neck. Michelle was traveling down the wrong road fast.

She kept getting into fights at school—when she actually went. She no longer cared about her grades, but she wasn't stupid by any means. Michelle was very smart, which is why Cassey just couldn't understand her behavior. Must be runnin' with the wrong crowd.

On top of that, Michelle and Reggie were constantly fighting. Cassey always felt as if she had to referee or choose sides.

Cassey's relationship with Reggie was suffering for it, too. He was drinking too much and in a foul mood when he wasn't. She was actually beginning to think that he was messing around with other women.

She almost couldn't blame him. Who'd want to come home to this? There were days when Cassey herself just wanted to run away. But go where? And she had a daughter and a man that she had to care for. Shoot, without her, who knows what kinda mess they'd each get into?

Michelle sauntered back into the bedroom and grabbed her jacket.

"Where you think you going?" Cassey demanded. "I didn't say you could go nowhere."

"I'm just going next door to Nikki's."

"I don't want you hanging 'round that lil' thief."

"Nikki is my best friend."

"Then maybe you should find yo'self some better friends. That girl ain't been nothin' but a bad influence on you. Now she got you stealin'."

"Nikki didn't make me do anything. I did it because I wanted to. I wanted that shirt, so I took it."

Cassey put a hand to her chest and leaned against the door. "Lord, I don't know what to do with you."

"I'll be back later," Michelle announced.

"You better. We got to go to court in the morning."

"I haven't forgotten."

Michelle and Nikki had gotten busted for shoplifting at Dillard's department store. Now they had to go before the judge tomorrow morning. It would be a first offense for them both, so the court-appointed attorney didn't foresee anything other than probation.

But Cassey was getting to the end of her rope. She didn't know what to do.

When Michelle slammed out of the house Cassey simply hung her head and cried. Her family was falling apart and she just didn't know what to do.

After dropping Cassey off at the revival, Reggie went to find his own salvation.

As he weaved his way through the haze of a smoke-filled room, a woman approached him. "You need some comp'ny t'night, handsome?"

"Naw . . ."

"I . . . I can make . . . you happy," she promised through black lips. "Good to ya." She opened her shirt to reveal her breasts.

Disgusted, Reggie said, "Girl, hide them things. They wouldn't excite a dog on the street."

He navigated past a couple sleeping on the sofa in the living room, heading to the den. Reggie strode up to a group of people seated around a fifty inch big-screen television and found an empty spot to sit down.

They were passing a crack pipe.

"This way, Lil' Bit," Reggie said and gestured to the woman sitting beside him.

"Don't even think it," she uttered. "You better come up with that money."

"Ssssh." Reggie didn't have any money—he couldn't get any more out of Cassey this time. But his body was calling for crack. He had to have it, no matter the risk.

Reggie's eyes traveled over to a tall muscular man with a baby face standing in front of the black lacquer entertainment center going through a stack of CDs. He had his back to them for the moment, concentrating on whatever he was looking for. Dupree was his name and he wore a shoulder-harness holster and carried a pair of matching nine-millimeter guns. Reggie would just try to steer clear of him. Not call attention to himself. He owed him quite a bit of money, but Reggie couldn't stay away. He needed a fix.

Someone turned on the television and began switching channels. The telecast of the revival filled the screen and the preacher's loud voice bounced out of the speakers.

"Aww, please . . . the last thing I need is a guilt trip," Eli complained. "C'mon now . . ."

"My mama is somewhere at that revival," Dupree announced without turning around. "Anybody that got a problem with what's on the TV can just get out."

One guy named Scottie said, "Soon as I get off drugs, I'm gon' give my life to Jesus."

Eli chuckled. "I don't think Jesus is holding His breath."

"Outta ever'body in here smokin', I'm the only one that belongs," Scottie commented. He pointed to the petite woman sitting beside Reggie. "Lil' Bit, you need to be home with your three kids."

"You need to mind your own business."

Pointing, Scottie uttered, "Eli, you ain't no better."

"Don't go there, snaggletooth," Eli shot back.

Lil' Bit and Reggie busted up in laughter.

Reggie grabbed the pipe, taking the opportunity to fulfill his need.

"Yeah, my teeth fell out . . . ," Scottie admitted. "But you used to be the smartest kid on the block, Eli. You shoulda stayed in school or something, yo. You shouldn't be peddling no dope, man. Then you smokin' on top of that. How you livin', bro?"

"Y'all got somethin' for me, right?" Dupree interjected suddenly.

His words washed over Reggie because he was so consumed with the pipe. The only thought on his mind was the feeling that only getting high would bring.

Scottie gestured toward Reggie. "Yo' pay the man. . . . Old behind been smokin' so long Jheri curls done came, went, and on they way back again."

More laughter.

Dupree wasn't amused. His voice deepened. "Where my money, yo? I ain't got all night. Who got my money?"

Everyone avoided eye contact.

Dupree pulled out a gun.

Waving it in the air, he repeated his question. "I said, who got my money?"

Lil' Bit pointed at Reggie.

"You got something for me?" Dupree asked Reggie as he approached him.

Swallowing hard, Reggie responded, "Tomorrow. I'll have it tomorrow."

Dupree placed a gun to Reggie's head and cocked it. "Ain't no layaway here."

"Now wait a second, young bro. . . ." Reggie's voice quivered with fear. "You young enough to be my son."

Dupree's eyes traveled to the television.

Bishop Jakes was speaking to the congregation and the television audience.

"You have to choose your friends and make sure that they have had something die in their life. . . ."

"I'll tell you what," Dupree began. "I'll let God decide for you. Ain't but two bullets in here."

"C'mon, man. Don't do this," Reggie stammered in fear. "You ain't got to do this."

"I ain't doing nothing! You in God's hands."

Bishop Jakes looked straight into the camera. "If you've never had anything to go wrong in your life . . ."

Dupree pulled the trigger . . .

Click.

Icy fear twisted around Reggie's heart and his life flashed before his eyes. *Lord, please save me,* he prayed. *If you save me, I won't come back here no more.*

Dupree pulled the trigger a second time, intent on making an example out of Reggie. He couldn't let anyone think they could come smoke his crack and not pay. He wasn't running a charity— this was business.

Click.

Scared out of his wits, Reggie continued to plead for his life. "C'mon, Dupree. Give me a chance. I'll bring you yo' money. I swear I will. You ain't got to do this."

"If you've never had anything die in your life, don't counsel me . . . ," Bishop Jakes's voice boomed.

Dupree pulled the trigger again. *Click.*

In a sudden move, Reggie dropped to the floor; his flailing arms knocked the gun out of Dupree's hand.

Panic rioting within, he jumped to his feet and bolted for the nearest exit as fast as he could.

Crack—crack—crack . . .

Dupree was shooting at him.

Reggie ran faster.

Outside he dived for cover behind a thick bush.

"You got 'til tomorrow to get my money, old man," Dupree shouted from the doorway.

Reggie stayed in the bushes until he felt it was safe to leave. He couldn't control the spasmodic trembling within him.

"Help me, Lord," he prayed fervently. "Let me make it home safe . . . please . . . I beg you. Help me. . . ."

12

Michelle shifted in her seat and tried to focus on what Bishop Jakes was saying.

"... I personally don't like to have a whole lot to do with people who have not been through pain. It's nothing against them. I'm not jealous of them. I just can't relate to them. I can't relate to them and I am sure that they will not be able to relate to me."

As Bishop Jakes continued, Michelle looked over at Nicole and could tell from her body language that she was really taking in what the preacher was saying.

"The parts of me that I need to have known, that I need to have touched, that I need to have fellowship with, are tied up, not in the successes of my life, but in the struggles of my life."

Now what could this man know about struggles? Michelle thought. *He wanna know about struggles? I could preach to him on that.*

"For God has done more through my struggles than he's ever done through my successes. My successes are made out of the ingredients of my struggles. And you can never know my successes until you understand my struggles, because my struggles are the pathway that led me into my success. And your struggles will lead you to yours. Are you hearing what I'm saying?"

Bishop Jakes turned his gaze in her direction. It was almost as if he was looking directly at her.

Michelle averted her eyes, but could still feel the weight of his gaze, deep and probing.

"Your trials were your training camp, preparing you for greatness. You can let your troubles weigh you down like heavy bricks, or you can use those bricks as stepping-stones to a better place. Are you ready to lay your struggles down and walk all over them to get where they are leading you?"

Michelle moved restlessly in her seat. She had come to terms long ago with her life. But now Bishop Jakes's words aroused something within her, and it made her uncomfortable. Because whenever she began to hope for something better, it was like a wrecking ball came along and knocked her down and demolished her dreams.

"Come on, let's go," Michelle said, grabbing Nicole's arm.

"What you wanna leave now for? What's wrong?"

"Nothing," Michelle said. "I just wanna get out of here. I'm sore from today and I just want to go home."

Nicole eyed her friend warily, but agreed to leave. "You sure you okay?"

"I'm fine. Come on now."

Michelle was out of the sanctuary before Nicole could even get up. She just had to get out of there.

Cassey was back from revival and reading her Bible when Reggie came home.

She opened her mouth to ask about his disheveled appearance, but he just shook his head. He barely said a few words to her before heading to the bathroom to take a shower.

Cassey was in the hallway waiting for him when he came out. "You want to tell me what's going on?"

Reggie snapped, "Just give me a minute. Can I at least put some clothes on?"

Cassey knew something was up and she meant to find out what, but she went back to the living room to wait for him.

Reggie joined her a few minutes later. "Hey, Cassey. I'm sorry for talkin' to you like that. I just . . . I had somethin' on my mind."

She had a feeling by his nervous demeanor and the way he kept peeking out the window that something was deeply bothering him.

Cassie studied his face. "Reggie . . . are you okay?"

He nodded.

Suddenly he placed his hands to his face and broke down. "C-C-Cassey . . ."

"What is it, honey?"

Reggie sank down beside her. "Cassey, baby, I'm in trouble."

She laid a hand to his cheek, wiping away his tears. "Talk to me. . . . Tell me what's got you so upset." Cassey had been won-

dering if he'd gotten into gambling. Especially the way he was always asking for money.

"I . . . I . . . I . . ." He paused. "I . . . I need some money, but it
ain't just the money. My life . . . I've messed it all up. I don't know
what to do."

Reggie collapsed in her lap, weeping like a child.

Cassey was stunned—she'd never seen him act this way.

"Reggie, I don't know what's wrong," Cassey stammered in be-
wilderment, "but I know who can fix it."

He looked up at her and met her gaze. She'd never seen Reggie look so scared before.

"I'm so sorry. P-please don't leave me, C-Cassey. . . . Don't
leave me."

His behavior was making her uneasy. "Sorry for what, Reggie?" Cassey inquired. "What are you sorry for?"

Reggie wailed loudly, then buried his face in her bosom.

"It'll be okay. The last night of revival is tomorrow and I want
you to come with me. I don't know how, but God's gonna fix it."
Cassey began to rock Reggie in her arms. "It's gon' be all right,
honey. God can make all things right."

She and Reggie stayed like that for almost an hour.

Cassey pressed him for more answers but it was clear that he
was too distraught to talk, so she dropped her interrogation.

When the clock struck two in the morning, Cassey attempted
to stifle her yawn.

"Why don't you go on to bed," Reggie suggested.

"I wanna make sure you all right."

He nodded. "Go on . . . go to bed."

Cassey observed Reggie for a moment. "What's bothering you? Why won't you tell me?"

"I made a big mess of my life. I just don't know how to fix things . . . you know." Reggie eyed Cassey. "I don't want to lose you."

"I'm not going nowhere, honey. You just got to be honest with me, Reggie. All of us got to get our lives right with God."

"I hear what you saying, Cassey. I do." Reggie took her hand in his. "I know I haven't been real good to you all the time, but that's gonna change. I promise you."

Cassey stood up. "Reggie, why don't you come to bed with me. I know you're tired and you got a whole lot on yo' mind. We'll talk some more tomorrow morning."

"You go on," he insisted. "I'll be in there soon."

"Don't stay up too long."

"I won't," Reggie promised.

Troubled, Cassey watched him for a moment before making her way to their bedroom. She prayed for God to move on Reggie's heart. After what she witnessed tonight, Cassey was convinced that he was ready to accept Jesus into his life.

His cell phone pressed to his ear, Reggie peeked through the curtains for the fifth or sixth time. He was careful to keep his voice low so that Cassey wouldn't overhear. "I can get the money."

"*Can* ain't *got*," Eli stated. "Man, Dupree ain't playin' 'round. He'll kill you, Reggie. That young dude is crazy in the head."

Reggie stole a quick glance over his shoulder. "Did he say he was out lookin' for me?"

"He said he didn't care if you had to take the church offering money."

"I bet." Reggie glanced out the window a seventh time.

"You ever think about how much money gets passed around in that tray?" asked Eli.

"Naw, and to tell you the truth, I'm trying not to."

"It could get us out of a hole in a hurry," Eli suggested. "And the best part is—no one would ever miss it. Easy money. Think you could get Cassey to—"

"No, Eli," he interrupted. Reggie looked at the phone with disdain.

Putting it back to his ear, he questioned, "You tryin' to send me straight to hell, man?"

"Man, we already headed there. I'm just tryin' to avoid going tonight."

"I'ma get the money. You ain't got to worry 'bout it, Eli."

"Reggie, you coming to bed?"

At the sound of Cassey's voice, Reggie whispered, "Hey . . . gotta go. Talk to you tomorrow."

He hung up.

Reggie took another look before turning off the lights in the living room and walking into the bedroom.

Cassey was sitting up in bed waiting for him.

"I thought you'd be asleep by now," he muttered as he climbed into the bed with her.

"You had me worried 'bout you, Reggie."

"I told you I'ma be okay. I just need to pay off my debts." He looked over at her. "I really need your help with the money, Cassey. I'm in some real trouble."

"We'll talk 'bout all this in the morning."

Reggie lay down but couldn't sleep. He lay awake most of the night listening, in case Dupree showed up on his doorstep.

When he was sure Cassey was asleep, he crept out of bed and into the kitchen to retrieve a knife for protection.

Out of the corner of his eye, Reggie thought he saw something outside the kitchen window.

He dropped to the floor and crawled over to the back door.

With his ear pressed to the door, he listened.

Nothing except the loud thumping of his heart. Reggie swallowed hard.

When he heard nothing unusual, his heart returned to its normal pace.

Reggie stood up slowly.

Easing over to the window, he stared out, trying to detect anything out of place.

Reggie grabbed the butcher knife and headed back to the bedroom. He cursed himself for being so jumpy.

This was payback for Michelle. He was being paid back for all the sins he committed, Reggie decided.

I can be a better person, he kept telling himself. *I want to be a better person. I looked at my life tonight and I didn't like what I saw.*

Michelle stayed in the shadows as she crept around to the back of the house. Beneath the huge tree that used to hold a swing, she began digging in the dirt.

Every now and then she would stop and listen.

Biting her lip, Michelle returned her attention to her task. She didn't have to dig too far to find what she was looking for.

She pulled the bag out of the dirt and set it beside her.

Shoving soil back into the recently dug hole, she was suddenly anxious to escape from the disturbing presence of her childhood home.

Rising up, Michelle grabbed the bag and crept to the front of the yard.

She felt the hair on the back of her neck stand up, spurring her to walk faster—she wanted to put as much distance as possible between her and that house. She also didn't want to get caught out past curfew.

She had no idea that her appearance at the Jordan house had been witnessed.

"Like a thief in the night, I went back to that house, Bishop," Michelle stated, adding another matchstick to her house. "I needed to get the one tangible piece of my pain."

"Why did you wait until it was dark?"

"I didn't want anyone to know I'd ever been there. I had to sneak out of the halfway house and walk the whole way there. I didn't care though. It wasn't all that far."

Michelle broke into a small laugh. "You shoulda seen me tip-toeing across the street and into the backyard. My stomach was in knots the whole time I was back there digging in the dirt with my hands.

"I took out that old bag and put the dirt back down in that

hole, then got out of there. I practically ran all the way back to the halfway house. My chest felt like it was gonna burst, but that didn't make me slow down one bit. I just kept on running like somebody was after me."

"How did you get back in? Nicole?"

Michelle nodded. "Once I got back, I opened the bag and showed Nikki the dress."

"What happened?"

"She cried."

"How did you feel, Michelle? Seeing your dress again after all this time?"

"It was like having it happen to me all over again."

What was Michelle doing here in the middle of the night? Cassey wondered. *And what was she carrying?*

She didn't want to upset Reggie, so Cassey decided not to mention her daughter's nocturnal visit, but her thoughts were disquieting.

Cassey didn't hear Reggie when he entered the kitchen.

He placed both hands on her shoulders and guided her toward the doorway. "You go sit down. You've been working all morning."

She gave him a sidelong glance. "Go on and quit playin' with me."

"I'm serious. I haven't been appreciating you the way I should."

His words sent alarm bells ringing. "I ain't got no money, Reggie. Checks won't get cut until after the revival."

"I don't want any money." Reggie said the words tentatively, as if testing the idea. "Now go sit down."

Cassey turned around to face him. "What's got into you?"

"I don't know . . . ," Reggie responded. "Maybe God."

She folded her arms across her chest and asked, "Are you serious?"

"I've tried everything else. I gotta turn my life around."

Ecstatic, Cassey embraced Reggie. "Thank you, Jesus. Oooh praise Yo' name . . ."

He took a step away from her.

Taking a deep breath, he put his hands to his mouth.

He was wearing that same troubled expression that he had the night before.

"What is it?" Cassey asked, the worry returning.

He gave her a wry smile. "Things gotta change. . . ."

Reggie walked over to the sink and began washing the dishes. "Cassey, I want to be honest with you about some things. I did a lot of thinking last night and I want to be right."

"Yeah?" Her voice had drifted into a hushed whisper.

She chewed on her bottom lip and stole a look at Reggie.

"I been smoking dope. . . ."

Cassey's eyebrows rose in surprise. This was the last thing she'd expected to hear. "Reggie, you know how I feel about drugs. Then there's your diabetes. It's a wonder you haven't killed yo' fool self."

"I know, Cassey. But starting today, I ain't never touching no more crack. I'll go to rehab—do whatever I have to do."

"You mean it, Reggie?"

He nodded. "I do. I ain't never touching it again."

"Is that what you wanted to tell me?"

"That's part of it. If I'm gon' do this, I might as well come clean 'bout everything. I don't want no more secrets between us." Reggie took a deep breath. "Cassey, there have been some women over the years. But no more. I mean it 'bout changing. I want to be a better person. A better man."

She looked up at him with an effort. "That's all God wants."

"I just want a fresh start. Not just with God." Reggie reached over and took her by the hand. "I want to start over with you."

Cassey sighed with relief, "I'm so glad to hear you say this."

"It feels good—being honest with you like this."

Recalling the image of Michelle running away in the middle of the night, the nagging in the back of her mind refused to go away this time. "There's one more thing I need to know. I need the truth—no matter how much you think it may hurt me. Did you ever touch Michelle?"

Reggie stopped washing dishes. He dried his hands and turned to face her. "Cassey, I'm older now . . . my body is breaking down and I'm paying for a lot of things I did when I was young. Some of it, I wish I could take back. But that, Cassey . . . taking something that special from a child . . . That I could never do."

Relieved, Cassey fell into his arms, resting her head on his shoulder. "Thank you for being so honest."

13

Bishop Jakes shifted in his chair and looked around the jail cell. Such a small, dark place. But he knew this was nothing compared to the darkness that Michelle lived with all her life.

"It seems like you were confronting a lot of your past that weekend. Seeing your mother again. Holding that stained dress. It must have been difficult."

"My past has always been with me, Bishop," Michelle said, looking up at him. "I ain't never been able to escape it. Those three days at the revival just brought everything to a head."

"It makes me sad that you had no one you could talk to about what you were going through. If I had only known, we could've talked that weekend, Michelle. I wish I could have . . ."

"Bishop, don't sweat it. I always handled stuff on my own. My mama never protected me, Mama-Mary was useless—even God didn't protect me. I learned early on that I had to protect myself and it's one thing I became pretty good at. . . ."

"What's wrong, Michelle?" Nicole whispered as they walked home together from school. "You been real quiet lately. That ain't like you."

"Just dealing with some stuff at home."

"Your parents getting on you?"

Michelle shook her head. "I only have one parent, Nikki. Reggie ain't related to me in any kind of way."

"You don't like him much, do you?"

"I hate him," Michelle replied vehemently.

"I don't like him either."

Michelle glanced over at her friend. She grabbed Nicole by the arm. "Why don't you like him? Nikki, he done something to you?"

"Naw. It ain't nothin' like that."

They resumed their walking.

"I just don't like the way he looks at me," Nicole confessed. "And sometimes he winks at me when nobody's looking."

"He's a nasty pig." Michelle spat out the words.

Nicole stopped walking.

"Hey . . . did your stepfather . . . I mean Reggie . . . did he try to . . ."

Michelle took a deep breath, releasing it slowly.

Nicole continued to press her. "You can tell me. . . ."

Michelle needed to unburden her soul with someone. She and Nicole had been friends forever and shared many secrets. If she could trust anyone, it was Nicole.

They sat down on the curb in front of Nicole's house.

"Nikki, you have to promise you won't ever repeat anything I tell you."

"I won't. . . ." Nicole made an X across her chest. "Cross my heart."

Michelle sat there and confided in her best friend.

When she was done she pulled up her sleeves to show her the bruises he'd left on her body. "I got these from trying to fight him—keep him off me."

"So what did your mama say when she saw them?"

"She hasn't seen them."

"Why not, Michelle?"

"She doesn't believe me—she only listens to Reggie's lies."

"But you got those bruises on your arms—she's gotta believe you when she sees them."

"Cassey only sees what she want to see, Nikki. When it come to Reggie, she don't believe he'll do any wrong."

Nicole twisted her mouth into a frown. "That Reggie should be dead."

"One day I just might kill him," Michelle uttered.

"I'll help you," Nicole interjected. "We'll go to jail together and be roommates."

Michelle laughed. "I think it's called cellmates. But I don't want to go to jail. Reggie is the criminal—he should be locked away in some prison—not me."

"I still can't believe that you can't tell your mama. I mean, you got the bruises to prove it."

Michelle shook her head. "I'm telling you, Nicole. She won't believe me. She thinks I'm jealous of her time. Nothing else matters to Cassey except Reggie."

"What about Todd? Have you told him anything?"

Michelle looked horrified at the mere thought of Todd knowing anything about her and Reggie. "I can't tell him about this. And Nikki, you'd better not either. You promised. . . ."

"I won't say nothin'," Nicole vowed. "You know, Todd thinks you're mad with him or something. Are you?"

Shaking her head no, Michelle responded, "I just don't feel the same way anymore. I like him a lot, but . . ." She gave a slight shrug. "It's just not the same."

"Maybe we should run away from home," Nicole suggested.

"I know why I want to leave, but Nikki, why you want to run away?"

"I'm just tired of my mom's mouth. The woman is crazy."

Michelle shook her head and laughed. She laughed until tears rolled down her cheeks.

Cassey pulled up in front of their house and parked.

She got out of her car, shouting, "Michelle, I hope you done yo' homework already—you sittin' out here playin' around with Nicole over there."

Michelle muttered a curse and stood up. "I'll see you later, Nikki."

"Stay strong," she responded. "I'm here for you."

Michelle slowly made her way to her house.

Cassey was standing on the porch. "You just think who you are, huh? Takin' yo' own sweet time to get here. I'm 'bout sick of you."

Rolling her eyes, Michelle ignored her mother and headed straight to her room. She ran into Reggie in the hallway.

"Hey, Michelle . . . ," he greeted her. His eyes boldly traveled down to her breasts.

She released a string of curses.

Reggie glared at her. "You think you grown, don't you?"

"No," Michelle shot back. "You think I'm grown—that's why you always touching me," she added in a loud voice.

Reggie raised his hand and slapped her.

Michelle screamed.

Balling up her fists, she hit Reggie as hard as she could. He grabbed her wrists. "Oh, you like it rough now. . . ."

His voice changed as Cassey neared them. "Don't you ever talk to me like that again."

"What's going on?" She looked from Reggie to Michelle.

"He just hit me," Michelle shouted.

"She was being her ol' nasty self. She cursed at me."

Cassey stomped her foot in frustration. "Why can't I just have some peace in my house? I'm so tired of all this mess."

Michelle stalked off to her bedroom, vowing to leave that house as soon as she was able.

Michelle and Nicole sat on the porch of the halfway house.

"I really appreciate you letting me in last night."

Nicole swatted her playfully on the arm. "You just lucky you came back when you did—I was hardly able to keep my eyes open any longer."

Michelle took a sip of her coffee. "I couldn't wait to leave that house."

Nicole nodded in understanding.

Michelle took another sip and thought about what she was about to do tonight.

Nicole interrupted her thoughts. "Your bruise is healing up."

"Still hurts, though," she responded and touched her face. "I wish I could make Pervis look like this. I know one thing—I'ma be ready the next time."

"Yeah, but we gotta keep our noses clean so that we can get outta here."

Michelle agreed.

"That was something else last night."

Puzzled, Michelle questioned, "What was?"

"That service. The singing. The dancing. All that. It reminded me of when we were little. Remember Sunday school, Michelle? How you used to sing. You were so good. You still sing?"

Michelle spied a car slowly approaching.

When the car came to a halt across the street, she squinted in order to get a look at the driver.

". . . 'Mean Old World' . . . that was the song you used to sing. I loved that song."

"Let's go," Michelle uttered as she jumped to her feet.

She grabbed Nicole's arm and began walking.

They left the halfway house and headed down the street, walking fast.

"What?" Nicole questioned. "Why you in such a hurry?"

"Pervis."

Sheer fright washed over Nicole's face. "He's gonna kill me, Michelle."

"C'mon. I'm not gon' let that happen."

Michelle and Nicole turned down a side street, hoping to avoid another confrontation with Pervis. They both jumped at the sound of a car coming to a screeching halt on the street beside them.

Todd rolled down the window and said, "I didn't mean to startle you. You two need a ride?"

Michelle put up a hand to hide her face, but Todd glimpsed it anyway.

"What happened?" His look of concern almost broke Michelle's heart.

She tossed a glance over her shoulder and saw that Pervis had followed them. He winked and blew her a kiss.

"Yeah, we need a ride," Michelle answered quickly.

She pulled open the car door and got inside while Nicole climbed into the backseat.

"What happened to your face?" Todd inquired a second time.

"Nothing you need to worry 'bout, Todd. Just a little accident."

"Are you okay?"

"Well . . . ," Nicole began.

Michelle shot her a look to silence her. "I'm okay."

Todd was not about to let up. "Who did that to you, Michelle? I know it wasn't no little accident like you said. Do you need me to handle it?"

"I said I was all right," Michelle stated in a tone that brooked no argument. "I can take care of myself, Todd."

Todd—he was always trying to be her protector.

Michelle's mind traveled back to the past to another time when her friend tried to be her hero.

"Where you get all them bruises?" he asked her, one day after they were playing around, wrestling.

Embarrassed, Michelle snatched her arm away from Todd. "Ain't nothing."

"What happened?" he pushed. "Who did that to you?"

"I said it ain't nothing," Michelle snapped in anger.

She tried to step around him, but Todd blocked her exit.

"Why you always running away, Michelle?"

She shoved him with all her might. "Todd, you need to mind yo' own business and leave mine alone. I don't need you to help me."

"Hey . . . you don't have to be so mean," he yelled at her. "I'm just trying to be your friend."

"Leave me alone, then."

Michelle ran away as fast as her legs would take her.

She didn't see the car parked in front of the house and sighed with relief. Reggie wasn't home.

Michelle crept into the house, hoping to get past her mother. She didn't want to deal with Cassey getting on her case about her room.

"Where you been? Probably down there with that ol' nasty boy."

Michelle glanced over her shoulder. "I was outside," she responded.

"Your room is a mess," Cassey stated, her mouth twisted in a frown. "You better get yo' fast behind in there and clean it up."

Filled with rage, Michelle turned on her mother. "You clean it—you want it cleaned so much."

Cassey was taken aback. Her mouth dropped open in her shock. "W-what did . . . what did you say to me?"

Michelle didn't blink an eye. "You heard me. I'm tired of you on my back."

"Girl, you better wash yo' mouth. I oughta backhand ya—"

"I don't care what you do to me. It can't be any worse than having to live here in this house with you and Reggie."

Cassey's eyes grew wet with her tears. "I do the best I can for you and this . . . th-this is how you treat me?" She shook her head in dismay.

Michelle eyed her mother, feeling guilty over her outburst. "You always yelling at me like I'm a dog," she complained. "Why can't you talk to me like I'm a person?"

"I wouldn't have to talk to you any kind of way if you'd do what you told, Michelle. And I do too much for you to sass me like that."

"If you want respect, then you need to give me some respect, too."

Cassey wiped at her eyes. "All right. Michelle, I would like for you to clean yo' room, please. I would also like for you to try and keep it clean. Do you think you can do that for me?"

"Okay," she muttered.

Michelle turned away from Cassey and walked into her bedroom, locking the door behind her. It didn't matter about the lock because it no longer worked since Reggie broke it.

She'd tried to lock him out of her room, but he'd managed to make it inside anyway. There was no escaping him.

Not now, but Michelle vowed one day she would.

One day she would make Reggie pay for what he'd done to her.

"Every time I thought I was free of Reggie, there he was again."

"What do you mean?" Bishop Jakes asked.

"I'd left home. Was living on the streets for a while then met Pervis. Actually, I knew him but then we got together."

Bishop Jakes nodded in understanding.

"Anyway, Pervis got me hooked on crack and then wanted me to start stripping. Said I owed him all this money. I did it. That's when I ran into Nicole again. I hadn't seen her for a while. She'd run off with Bobby and got married 'cause she was pregnant."

Michelle shifted her position on the floor of the cell.

"So I was working as a stripper. I'd been doing it for about eight months." As she talked, Michelle's mind took her back to the day Reggie reappeared in her life.

She swung around the pole, her senses dulled by booze and drugs.

Michelle moved to the music as she tantalized and teased the patrons in the packed strip club.

She bent down, giving some man a close-up view of her breasts.

Michelle moved only after he stuffed money in her skimpy top. She then sashayed on to her next victim.

"C'mere, girl," Michelle heard a familiar voice call out to her.

Unnerved, she looked out into the crowd for the face the voice belonged to—Reggie.

Michelle glanced over to the corner where Pervis conducted business. She felt a shred of relief seeing him there. For now, he was her protection against Reggie, if need be.

"Take off your clothes," another voice shouted. "I wanna see some skin."

Michelle was beginning to think she'd imagined Reggie's voice when she heard it again.

This time the voice seemed closer, but when she looked into the crowd, she still didn't see him. Maybe it was the pills she'd taken.

She tried to lose herself in the music, hoping to erase Reggie's voice from her mind. Michelle moved faster, seducing men with her body.

She flirted with her eyes and her sexy smile, but when her routine ended, she rushed off the stage without looking back.

Nicole was preparing to go on.

Handing Michelle a robe, she commented, "Girl . . . you hear that? They want you to do an encore."

Michelle muttered a curse and kept on walking to the dressing room.

As soon as she walked into the room, Michelle had a strong feeling she wasn't alone.

Her eyes landed on the lone figure standing near the window.

"What are you doing back here?" she demanded, her eyes filled with hatred.

Michelle hadn't seen Reggie in over a year. The last time was when she walked out of her mother's house.

After a big argument over her growing drug use, Michelle just packed up her possessions and left. She eventually moved in with Pervis and dropped out of high school. After getting her hooked on crack, Pervis soon had Michelle working at the club. Drugs and stripping—a deadly combination.

"I came to see you." Reggie gave her a lusty look. "Figured you'd give me a private lap dance."

"Get out of here before I call security."

Reggie took a step toward her. "Why you wanna act like that? You ain't glad to see me? It's been a while. Heard you was down here taking off yo' clothes—figured I'd come and see for myself. I been missing you, girl."

"Why don't you go on home to Cassey," Michelle suggested as her eyes swept the length of the room, looking for a way to escape.

"You can't tell me you haven't been thinkin' 'bout me. You won't let yo'self admit it, but we good together."

Michelle's gaze landed on the knife they'd used earlier to cut Nicole's birthday cake.

She moved slowly toward it, hoping that Reggie hadn't noticed it.

When it appeared he hadn't, she set out to keep him distracted.

Giving him a sexy smile, Michelle opened her robe. "This what you wanna see?" she asked him.

Reggie grinned. "Yeah . . . I knew in time you'd welcome it."

Michelle walked slowly until she was within arm's reach of the knife.

She removed the robe. "What you waitin' for? This is why you're here, ain't it?"

Reggie pounced on her.

He was so caught in his lust that he didn't see her grab the knife. Michelle stabbed him in the chest.

He screamed and she laughed.

"You won't ever touch me or nobody again," she said gleefully and tried to stab him a second time.

"Hey, Michelle . . ."

Nicole's voice summoned her out of her slumber.

She opened her eyes and sat up in bed. "Huh? I'm sorry, I must have fallen asleep. What did you say?"

"I asked if you're scared?"

Michelle thought about Nicole's question and shook her head. "Naw. I can't die but once."

"Well, I'd rather it be later than sooner," Nicole admitted. "I ain't ashamed to say I wanna see my kids again. I wanna see them grow up."

"You will," Michelle reassured her. "Pervis just tryin' to scare us."

"Good thing Todd came when he did, huh?"

Michelle shrugged nonchalantly. "Wouldn't of made a difference. I got my own back."

"I figure we don't need no more close calls like that. We need to look out for ourselves."

Michelle agreed.

"Look under your pillow."

Michelle hesitated.

"Did you look?"

"Just a sec." She slipped her hand under her pillow and pulled out a gun. "Where'd you get this? You crazy?"

"Look, I got it from an old friend. He owed me. I'm scared, Michelle. You know Pervis; no telling what he'd do. But I don't know how to handle it. I was hoping you did in case we run into some more trouble."

Examining the gun, Michelle murmured, "Or in case trouble runs into us."

Much to Michelle's disappointment, Reggie's wounds weren't life threatening. He pressed charges against her, despite Cassey's efforts to get him to reconsider. At least that was her mother's version of it, anyway.

Michelle wasn't sure if Cassey had tried hard enough but it didn't matter. The assault coupled with the drugs found in her purse and in the dressing room landed her a prison sentence.

Initially, she wasn't bothered by having to go to prison. Michelle considered it a much-needed break. She was away from Reggie and Pervis both. She no longer had to deal with either one of them.

Twana rarely missed a visiting day, while Cassey she rarely saw. Michelle didn't expect much from her mother, and she wasn't disappointed.

She did receive the occasional letter, and Michelle responded. Neither one of them mentioned Reggie.

Right after Michelle was sent to prison, Cassey found God, so she included scriptures and had even sent her a Bible one Christmas.

Michelle gave the Bible to another inmate, who had gotten

saved. She didn't see much point in keeping it—she wasn't going to read it, nor did she believe she had any reason to do so.

After God had allowed Reggie to treat her so badly, Michelle didn't want anything to do with Him. He'd abandoned her and now her life had become so unworthy of God's love—it was too late for her.

For a period, Cassey didn't write.

Twana would mention in her letters that Cassey sent her love, missed her, loved her. Michelle figured her godmother was simply trying to keep her from feeling rejected.

It was way too late for that, Michelle decided.

Then the letters started again. Cassey's writing had changed some, but Michelle was glad to hear from her mother.

Neither of them mentioned the lapse of time between letters. They both just pretended it never happened.

"Looking back I think the reason I didn't hear from my mother was because she'd had that stroke and couldn't write me."

"Why do you think they kept the news of Cassey's stroke from you?"

Shrugging, Michelle responded, "I don't know, Bishop. You'd have to ask them. Maybe my mother was embarrassed or somethin'. I can't really say."

"How did you feel when you found out?"

"Worried. Guilty. Left out. I was hurt that she didn't tell me. Mad that Twana didn't tell me about it either. After all, I was Cassey's daughter."

14

"You know what the worst part of this whole thing is, Bishop? I actually was starting to think that things could change." Michelle wiped a tear from her eye before it fell.

Bishop Jakes held out the box of tissues again, but Michelle waved it away.

"I guess it was all that talk of Jesus and forgiveness. You're good when you get to preachin', you know?" Michelle chuckled.

"Thanks," Bishop Jakes said and returned the smile.

"I kinda felt like there was a possibility that I could stop this downward cycle my life has been on and make things good . . . or at least better."

"It's never too late for that, Michelle."

"Aw, come on, Bishop. You good, but not *that* good. After all I've been through, no way I can buy that now."

Michelle picked up another matchstick, contemplating where to place it, but then looked up.

"But I have to admit, those couple of days, it felt nice."

"What did, Michelle?"

"Thinking that things could change. . . ."

"I talked to Bobby right before we left the house. That's who called me. He's gonna bring the kids tonight to revival," Nicole announced as she and Michelle walked to Twana's salon. "I'm so excited. I don't even know what to wear."

"Just wear that smile of yours. That's all you need."

Without warning, Nicole suddenly stopped dead in her tracks.

"What's wrong?" Michelle followed her gaze.

Pervis was walking toward them.

"C'mon, let's go," Nicole said, grabbing her arm.

Michelle held up her hand. "Hold up. I'm too old to run."

"I'm lookin' at two dead crackhead hos," Pervis stated in a deadly tone.

Unafraid, Michelle reached into her purse and fingered the gun. She kept her eyes on Pervis and then looked behind him. "That's funny. I'm looking at one stupid niggah and two live policemen."

She removed her hand from her purse and began to wave. "Morning, officers," Michelle greeted them sweetly.

Pervis glanced around and saw the two cops involved in a traffic stop across the street.

Turning back around, he grinned. "See y'all at church."

"Yeah. Whatever," Michelle muttered.

He moved on, leaving them trembling.

"I thought you was gonna shoot him. Right in front of the cops."

"I did, too," Michelle confessed. "Maybe next time. Let's go. We're gonna get you hooked up."

They walked another three blocks to Twana's hair salon.

As soon as Michelle walked in, Twana gasped in shock. "Girl, what happened to your face?"

"Slipped in the shower, that's all."

Twana's expression clearly showed she didn't believe Michelle's lie, but she did not refute it. "Well, look it here . . . Pumpkin! We're gonna need a little extra cover-up for Michelle tonight."

"I want you to do me up this time, too," Nicole interjected.

Twana chuckled. "Girl, we don't sell miracles here."

"Her husband called," Michelle explained. "He's coming to revival tonight. Even bringing the kids."

Twana gave Nicole a high five. "*Praise God.* Why didn't you say so? Then we'll need to make an exception now, won't we?"

"I want to look just like Michelle. How much will that be?"

"Ain't that much money in the world . . . ," Twana muttered. "Pok Chu, put my tape in from the service last night. That place was on fire."

"Yeah, it was . . . ," Nicole murmured.

"I don't get it," Michelle stated. "I see a lot of hoopin' and hollerin'. I see people givin' their hard-earned money to a preacher. I see much inspiration and perspiration, but what's the end result? You come right back home to the same old stuff."

Pok Chu turned on the television and hit the Play button on the VCR.

Michelle heard the familiar voice of Bishop Jakes. "There is something about going through death and loss and pain and misfortune and adversity. There is something about going through things that don't seem fair to you."

"That's right," Twana uttered in agreement. "God gives us the power to change the world. But I can't do that until I change myself. I know I left that service a changed woman. Turn that up, Pok Chu."

Several people shouted "Amen" around the salon.

Michelle carefully considered Bishop Jakes's words.

"Once you go through it, you need to make sense of the madness in your life. Since you can't change what happened and you can't alter what you've been through, at least you need to be able to think that there's some greater good that's going to come out of it. It's what they call bringing closure. To bring closure to it; to justify that I didn't go through this kind of pain for nothing, I need to be able to feel like something good is going to come out of this. If I can't do that, then I feel like I'm a victim. . . ."

I don't want to be a victim, Michelle whispered in her head. *Never again.*

Michelle was caught up with the tape when the salon door opened and in walked Todd. She was pleasantly surprised to see him, but she hoped he wouldn't start asking her about the black eye again. He asked too many questions and she knew he wouldn't give up.

"You got company, girl," Twana announced with a big grin. "Hi, Todd."

"Hey, Twana," he greeted. "Michelle . . ."

Patting Michelle on the back, Twana murmured, "I'll leave you two to talk."

Gesturing toward the door, Todd asked, "Can we take a walk?"

Michelle looked over to where Nicole was sitting. "You gonna be okay?"

"She's in good hands with Allstate," Twana assured her. "Now get on outta here."

Michelle and Todd left the salon and headed for a nearby park. No sooner had they reached the corner than Todd looked at her and asked, "You sure you okay?"

Michelle was getting exasperated. "How many times I got to tell you?"

He held up his hands in defeat. "Okay. Okay. I ain't trying to start nothin'." Todd paused a moment. "I don't know how else to say this other than to just say it. Michelle, I've never gotten over you. I never want to get over you."

She stopped walking. "I think we're good friends, Todd."

"What do I need to say to convince you?"

"Of what?"

"My feelings for you."

She couldn't let him finish. "Todd, look . . . my mind is just really screwed up right about now. Even if I could . . . I need to just focus on myself for a little while. . . ."

"I can respect that. But I want you to know that I'm not going anywhere. You won't be able to get rid of me so easily this time around."

Michelle looked away. She didn't want Todd to see just how much his words affected her.

They resumed their walking until they reached the park.

Todd questioned, "Remember when we were little?"

"To be real honest, no."

A ball rolled toward them, stopping at Michelle's feet.

A little girl came over to retrieve it. Locking eyes with Michelle, she smiled and said, "Hello."

Michelle pasted on a smile in return.

Running over to Todd, she requested, "Watch me sing, Daddy."

He grinned. "Okay, but stay close to your grandmother, Mia."

"No way . . . ," Michelle murmured.

"Yes way. Time flies."

"Little Sally Walker, sittin' in her saucer . . . Rise, Sally, rise. Wipe your weepin' eyes."

Michelle's eyes locked into Mia's, recalling a glimmer of what her life was like before Reggie destroyed her world.

"Put your hands on your hip and let your backbone slip. Ahhh . . . shake it to the east . . ."

Michelle mouthed the words as her body swerved slightly in rhythm. "Ahhh . . . shake it to the very one that you love the best."

Todd clapped. "That was great, honey."

Michelle clapped as well. "Yes, it was."

The girl ran to her grandmother and Michelle turned to Todd. "You're very lucky."

"The prayers of a righteous man availeth much."

She gave him a puzzled look. "*Availeth?* Is that even a word? If Jesus were here now, would He be talkin' like that or would He say, 'Y'all trippin' down here'?"

Todd threw back his head and laughed. "You're one of a kind, Michelle."

"I'm just being real."

"This is one of the things I really miss about you—your sense of humor."

Shrugging, Michelle responded, "Ain't had a whole lot to laugh about lately."

"I have a strong feeling all that's gonna change for you real soon."

Michelle eyed Mia. "Maybe. . . ."

Turning her attention back to Todd, she murmured, "I'd better head back to the beauty shop. I need to get my hair done for revival."

"I'll walk you back," he began,

Michelle took a step backward. "No, stay here with your daughter. I'll be all right walking by myself."

"I'll save you a seat next to me at church tonight."

Holding up two fingers, she said, "You better save two. Nicole is coming to church with me tonight. Her family's coming but I don't know if she'll be able to sit with them."

"Anything for you," Todd murmured.

"Whatever you say." Michelle surprised herself when she broke into a big grin.

"Mom, there's something wrong in Michelle's house. She has these bruises on her arm and she never smiles anymore."

"Todd, what you talkin' about?"

"I think her mama or her stepdaddy is beating on her or something."

His mother came over and sat down beside him. "Look, son . . . it's not nice to interfere in other folks' business. I don't know what Michelle is tellin' you, but we have to stay out of it."

"She didn't tell me anything, Mom. Every time I ask her something, she just gets mad with me and she runs away. She won't tell me a thing."

"Well, she don't want you in her business then."

Embracing him, his mother said, "Honey, I know you want to help Michelle, but this is not your fight. She will have to find her own way. . . ."

Todd hadn't had that particular memory in a long time.

Maybe it was seeing Michele with the bruise on her face that triggered the recollection. He recalled a feeling of helplessness—he still felt that way even now.

Todd just couldn't make sense of why it was so hard for him to make Michelle see that she didn't have to battle her demons alone. Todd loved her then and his feelings still hadn't changed.

His daughter ran up to him. "Daddy, I want ice cream."

Laughing, Todd pulled out a dollar bill and handed it to Mia. "Be careful," he warned.

"Wasn't that Michelle Jordan?" his mother asked when Todd took a seat beside her.

He nodded.

"You need to leave that girl alone, Todd. She got too many problems."

"I care a great deal for her, Mom. The way I see it—too many people have given up on her. I won't do that. Michelle thinks she's all alone in this world and I intend to make sure she knows that she has me."

15

"The last night of revival, I took a nice long bath and took my time getting dressed. It was going to be an important night for me, Bishop." She laughed. "I guess it was, huh? Just not in the way I thought."

"What were your expectations of that night, Michelle?"

"I wanted God to wash me clean of my sins and save me. I wanted Him to take away my shame and all that had happened to me. I wanted to give my life over to Him." Michelle picked up a matchstick. "But everything just went up in flames, I guess you can say."

She glanced over at Bishop Jakes. "I had no idea that I wouldn't make it. I think I surprised myself just as much as I surprised everyone else."

. . .

Michelle stared at her reflection in the mirror. Except for the slight visible bruising, she looked great, and she was looking forward to tonight.

Last night Bishop Jakes had requested that everyone bring to the service this evening whatever it was in their life that kept them bound to the world.

Michelle stared at the bundle lying on her bed. It wasn't very big but it was enough to prevent her from becoming the woman she could have been. She was tired of holding on to all of the hurt and anger. Michelle was ready to move forward in her life.

For the first time in a very long time, she felt hopeful. She truly believed that after tonight her life would be changed for the better.

An image of Todd formed in her mind, bringing a smile to her lips. She cared for him a great deal, but she wouldn't allow her emotions to drag him into her drama. He was a good man—she knew that much.

A good man deserves a good woman, her heart whispered.

She ran her fingers through her curls as she continued to admire herself in the mirror. "One day, Todd . . . ," she whispered.

Nicole burst into the room. "Do you think I really look okay?"

Michelle turned away from the mirror to check out Nicole's hair and makeup. "Girl, you look great."

"I just want Bobby to see how much I've changed, you know? I want to make my kids proud of me."

"You've succeeded. Nikki, you look beautiful."

Dropping down on her bed, Nicole inquired, "So what did you and Todd talk about? Y'all were gone for a good little while."

"You so nosy."

"Yeah. So are you gonna tell me or not?" Nicole admired her manicure. "Girl, he's in love with you."

Michelle rested her hands on her hips. "Why you say that?"

"Have you been paying any attention to the man?" Nicole questioned. "All you got to do is just look at him. He's got these big puppy-dog eyes whenever he sees you."

Michelle chuckled.

"He does. Just look at him. You'll see."

"I told him that I need to get myself together first, Nikki. Right now I ain't no good to nobody—not even myself."

Michelle dropped down on the edge of her bed. "I'm so screwed up."

"You got to change your way of thinkin'."

"Can't do it overnight," Michelle replied. "Gonna take some time. I been this way a while."

"One day at a time," Nicole contributed. "That's all we gotta do."

Michelle picked up the bag and pressed it to her chest. "One day at a time," she murmured to herself.

"I can't believe I'm gonna finally get to see my children tonight. I'm so excited."

Michelle laughed at her friend. "I can see that."

"I'm gonna make them so proud of me."

"I know you will," replied Michelle. "You really ain't got a thing to worry about, Nikki. When Bobby sees you, he's gon' know you on the way back."

"It's not that I'm looking for him to take me back or any-thing—I mean, I messed up big time, you know. I just want to be able to spend time with my kids—that's really all I want."

"But what if Bobby wants you back?"

"Then my life will be perfect," Nicole said with a laugh. Her face suddenly grew solemn and her smile disappeared. "You think Pervis gonna show up?"

"Where? At the church?"

She nodded. "That's what he said, remember? That he'll see us at the cathedral."

Michelle gave a slight shrug. "I don't know. He might. The man is crazy."

"So, what'll we do? I don't want my children to get hurt, you know?"

"You don't have to worry 'bout that," Michelle reassured Nicole, patting her purse.

"Michelle, you can't get caught with that gun."

"I won't, Nikki," Michelle promised. "I'll have it just in case we need it, but I'd really be surprised if Pervis shows up. Too many witnesses."

Nicole wasn't as convinced. "He may be waiting for us outside somewhere."

"Then we just have to keep our eyes open, that's all." Michelle smiled. "I'm not gon' let that stupid fool keep you from seeing your children, Nikki."

Michelle groaned when she heard Delores calling her name. "I wonder what she wants now."

Nicole chuckled. "Maybe you didn't wash the dishes right. You know how picky she is."

"She better not be calling me about something stupid like that," Michelle fumed. "I ain't in the mood. . . ."

"Reggie, you ready to go?" Cassey called from the living room. "We need to be leavin' here soon."

He stood in front of the full-length mirror in their room buttoning his shirt. "I think I'ma just drop you off. I don't feel like being 'round all those people tonight."

"No you don't," Cassey fussed. "Reggie, you promised to come to revival with me tonight. I'm gon' hold you to it."

He groaned.

"Did you hear me?"

"Yeah, I heard you, and so did everybody else on Lockhart Avenue," Reggie replied. "I'll be out in a minute." He fumbled with his tie, muttering something unintelligible.

Surveying himself in the mirror, he felt the tie still didn't look right.

Sighing in frustration, Reggie undid it and attempted to tie it again. He didn't know why he was so nervous about going to revival. It had been a long time since he'd stepped inside a church, but it wasn't no cause for him to be acting so fidgety now.

Cassey appeared in the doorway. "What's taking you so long?"

He turned around, facing her. "I can't get this tie right."

"Let me try and do it," Cassey suggested as she walked up to him.

Reggie waved away her assistance. "You got that twisted hand. Ain't much you can do with it. I'll get it right."

He saw the wounded look on her face. "Cassey, you know I

didn't mean it in a bad way. . . ." Reggie held out his hands to her. "My hands . . . I can't stop trembling. . . ."

Concerned, she inquired, "Is something bothering you?"

"I just got this feeling—it's kinda strange . . . I feel like something's gonna happen tonight . . . I can't shake it, Cassey."

"You 'bout to give yo' life to the Lord, Reggie. That's what you feelin'. You 'bout to change yo' life . . . it's a big step." She peered at him intently. "You haven't changed yo' mind, have you?"

Reggie shook his head no. "I haven't."

He turned back to the mirror. "I need to get this tie right. I can't go out there looking any kinda way."

Reggie swallowed hard, trying to wash away the anxiety he felt. He tried to keep his expression blank as he worked with his tie. He could feel the heat of Cassey's gaze on him.

Finally, he had the tie exactly the way he wanted it. Reggie turned back to Cassey. "See, that's better."

His eyes traveled the length of her body, then back up to her face. "You look real pretty, Cassey." He pointed to her hat. "That's a real nice touch."

She flushed. "I'm not used to you being so complimentary."

"I wronged you in a whole lotta ways, Cassey. But starting now, I'm gon' make it all up to you. Everything. I promise."

"You don't have to make promises to me, Reggie."

"You been good to me. I know that, Cassey. I—"

She placed a finger to his lips to silence him. "We fine, Reggie. Ain't nothin' for you to worry 'bout. Now, let's head on out to church. We wanna get some good seats tonight."

Reggie nodded. "I'm ready."

Cassey took him by the hand. "Let's go, honey."

Outside, Reggie turned to check out the house. Something about it seemed different, but he couldn't put his finger on it. His eyes searched around, looking for what? He had no idea.

"Reggie?" Cassey prompted.

"Here I come," he uttered.

Reggie discreetly surveyed his surroundings, making sure there was no sign of Dupree. He worried that the guy would show up on his doorstep. He had this vision in his head of walking out the door and Dupree jumping from behind some tree or bush with his gun blasting.

"Who you looking for?" Cassey questioned.

"Nobody." Reggie stole a peek in the rearview mirror. "I ain't looking for nobody."

When he glanced over at her, Reggie could tell by the expression on her face that Cassey didn't believe him but, to his relief, she didn't plague him with more questions.

Reggie had never been so scared in his entire life. Maybe he was just being paranoid. A part of him wanted to confide in Cassey, but he didn't want to scare her. She would want to get the police involved, which would only make matters worse.

Once Dupree got his money, he would leave Reggie alone.

The money. Reggie had to figure out a way to get the money. He prayed Cassey would let him have it this one final time. He wasn't going to touch any more drugs so he wouldn't be needing to go through this again.

Reggie decided he was much too old to keep living on the edge like this. He was angry with himself for ever letting things get this far. He was disappointed in the way he'd lived his life.

He pulled into the parking lot of the cathedral and turned off the car. Instead of opening the door, Reggie just sat there, gathering his thoughts.

"You getting out?"

He nodded. "Just give me a minute, Cassey."

"Honey, what's wrong with you?"

"I just . . ." Reggie shook his head. "C'mon. Let's go inside."

"Everything gon' be fine, Reggie. I can't tell you how I know, but I do."

"I sho hope you right, Cassey."

Michelle sat on the bed with her purse wide-open.

She stared at the gun. She hoped Pervis wasn't stupid enough to try and attack them at church. *Lord, don't let it come to that.*

She covered the gun with the bundle and rushed down the stairs to get Nicole so they could head to revival.

On her way out, she bumped into a woman she didn't recognize.

"Excuse me," Michelle mumbled. She paused. "Who you here to see?"

The woman replied, "Hi, I'm looking for Michelle Jordan."

Michelle folded her arms across her chest. "And who are you?"

"Marie Rodgers, her new parole officer."

"What are you doing here? I've been calling in like I was supposed to do."

Assessing Michelle from head to toe, Ms. Rodgers responded, "Just have to check on my parolees face-to-face. Make sure they're okay."

"I'm fine. Thank you."

The parole officer pulled out a small notebook and began writing. "And you've met your activity requirement? I must admit one of the more unusual stipulations I've seen."

"Yep. The revival. Tonight is the last night. It's been pretty incredible so far. I think it's having a good impact on me."

"Hmmm . . . I bet."

"Excuse me?"

"Everybody that comes out of prison finds Jesus, Allah or the agnostic equivalent," Ms. Rodgers stated without emotion. "I've seen every trick in the book and a few more yet to be published. Let me check your house arrest band."

Michelle pulled up her ankle-length skirt and stretched out her leg for inspection.

Ms. Rodgers bent down. "Not the most complimentary accessory but a necessary one nonetheless."

"Don't bother me none," Michelle responded.

The parole officer rose to her full height after examining the band. Digging inside her bag, she pulled out a small cup in a clear plastic wrapper.

Michelle's frown deepened. "I can't believe you pullin' this on me now."

"As part of your parole, you realize that you're subject to mandatory surprise drug testing."

She glanced over at the clock before taking the cup. "I'm clean, Ms. Rodgers. Can't we do this tomorrow or something? I'm supposed to be heading out on my way to church."

"You have a history of drug use. You served time for drug possession and—"

Michelle snatched the cup away from Marie. "Okay . . . whatever. . . ."

Nicole rushed into the room. "Girl, what's—" Her voice dropped when she saw Marie Rodgers.

"Nikki, you don't have to wait for me. I'll meet you at the church."

Nicole gave her a skeptical look. "You sure? I don't mind waitin' on you."

Michelle knew that Nicole was afraid of running into Pervis, but she suspected that the desire to see her husband and kids would override that fear.

Michelle nodded. "I'll see you there."

Ms. Rodgers eyed Nicole in silence.

"Okay. I'll see you later, Michelle."

"The sooner you pee in that cup, the sooner you can leave for revival," Ms. Rodgers reminded her.

"Ms. Rodgers, it ain't that I'm afraid to take the test. I just don't want to be late for revival. It's important to me—whether you believe it or not."

"Don't take that tone with me, Ms. Jordan. I've been doing this a long time and I know how it is. Do you know how many parolees get sent back because they violate their parole? The odds aren't in your favor."

Michelle's ire was up. "Ms. Rodgers, you act like you're just waiting for me to mess up."

The parole officer was losing her patience. "Let me check your purse."

"What?"

"Your purse, Ms. Jodan; give me your purse."

Michelle felt panic rise within her, but what choice did she have? She held out her handbag and chewed on her bottom lip.

"You do realize that any drugs, paraphernalia or firearms will be a violation of your parole?" Ms. Rodgers stated as she opened the purse.

She held up part of something bloodstained, her nose turned upward. She demanded, "What is this?"

"Bishop Jakes asked everyone to bring in a tangible symbol of something that has kept them bound to the past. That's the dress I was wearing the first time I was molested by my mama's boy-friend."

Michelle paused a moment before continuing. "I want to move forward in life without having to look back, Ms. Rodgers. After listening to Bishop Jakes, I know that even after all I been through, I can have a better life because I deserve better."

Ms. Rodgers stared down at the dress stained with dirt and blood, then back up at Michelle.

Without a word, she handed the purse back to Michelle. "I don't want to keep you any longer. You can do your urine test later."

Michelle released an audible sigh of relief when Ms. Rodgers left the house. She clutched the purse to her chest and walked out.

She wanted to make it to the church before the service started.

16

"You gotta believe," Bishop Jakes's voice boomed. "You gotta believe that the Lord will deliver you from your current situation. You gotta believe He will provide."

Todd looked around the sanctuary. There seemed to be more people here than there had been the last two nights. People were crowding the aisles and standing along the back. A few people glared at the empty seat beside him, but he was saving it for Michelle.

Every few minutes, Todd glanced around the sanctuary, looking for her. She was supposed to be here by now.

His mother leaned over and whispered, "Who you keep looking for?"

"Michelle. She's supposed to sit with us this evening."

He'd noticed Nicole when she entered the sanctuary fifteen

minutes ago. She was seated with her family just a few rows away.

Todd checked his watch.

Where was Michelle?

He was getting worried.

When the choir stood up to sing, he glanced around again. Still no sign of Michelle.

His mother leaned forward and whispered, "Stop worrying so. She'll be here. She's probably just running late."

He nodded in agreement. He didn't know why, but he had a bad feeling and he couldn't seem to get rid of it. He was edgy.

Every now and then, Todd caught Nicole checking out the sanctuary as well. He knew she was looking for Michelle, too. He thought about slipping out and going to look for her. Todd decided to give her another ten minutes. If she didn't arrive by then, he was definitely going to look for her.

He tuned in to Bishop Jakes's words. ". . . And if it takes too much sweat I don't need it. Stop begging people to stay. Let them go."

Todd had to wonder if those particular words weren't meant for him in regards to Michelle. Was he supposed to just let her go?

He shook his head. No. He couldn't just let Michelle go like that—she meant too much to him and he had a feeling she felt the exact same way about him. He'd never been able to get her to admit it, however.

Todd checked his watch. Michelle had another six minutes to arrive before he went looking for her.

He was still bothered by the bruises he'd seen on her face. Someone had beaten her—who? Todd wondered.

Michelle had attached herself to some rough characters after she ran away. . . .

Fear slithered down his spine.

Had Michelle run away again? Todd glanced down at his watch and was about to get up when his mother tapped him on the thigh and whispered, "She's here. I just saw her."

Relieved, Todd settled back in his seat.

Reggie fidgeted in his seat beside Cassey.

His attention kept jumping from Bishop Jakes to Dupree to Cassey—it was all over the place.

As he listened to the sermon, Bishop Jakes's words summoned memories Reggie wasn't willing to face at the moment.

". . . I feel like I've been victimized and I forever feel sorry for myself and I'm not free to go on with my life. And I'm not safe to remarry again, and I'm not safe to get another job again, and I'm not safe in another church again, because I have unresolved issues out of my past. And I'm not ready to go forward with life because I'm still tied up with where I came from."

Reggie felt a sudden urge to propel himself out of his seat and leave. He didn't want to be there.

As if Cassey had read his mind, she reached over and covered his trembling hand with her own.

I can't do this right now, he decided.

Reggie feared he was losing his mind; his heart started to pound faster and his chest felt like it was about to explode. He took several short breaths.

Cassey turned to face him. Her face was full of questions.

Reggie gave her a tiny smile. He didn't want to disappoint her again. He'd meant what he said about trying to be a better person. Feeling a sudden chill overtake his body, Reggie let his eyes travel around, looking for a sign of Dupree. The young dude was just crazy enough to gun him down right here in the church. He had to get Dupree his money. And soon. Reggie just needed some more time. Maybe if he could stay low-key for a few days—at least until Cassey could get her paycheck. This was going to be the last time he ever found himself in this position, Reggie vowed silently.

He sent up a quick prayer. *Dear Lord, keep me safe from Dupree. Please don't let him kill me. I'll do better. Amen.*

Reggie squeezed Cassey's hand to reassure her that all was okay with him.

Tonight he would do as he promised—he would give his life to the Lord. He had much to atone for.

Michelle stuck her head inside the sanctuary, looking around.

She saw the crowd and groaned in dismay at the thought of not being able to get inside. She didn't want to have to sit up in the balcony tonight. Biting her bottom lip in frustration, she ran her fingers through her hair.

Along with other visitors trying to get inside, Michelle stood for a few minutes in the foyer, listening to Bishop Jakes for a moment.

Recalling a side door, she made her way outside and into a side alley.

Eyeing a group of people walking through the door,

Michelle decided to follow them. She had to get inside the sanctuary tonight.

A worker stopped her, saying, "Employees only. You can't go through here."

"I'm with Cassey Jordan," Michelle stated. "She here yet?"

He looked her over.

"Cassey Jordan?" Nodding, he said, "Yeah, go ahead. Stop at the office and get a badge."

Michelle maneuvered through the pack of people milling about.

The worker caught up with her. "Office is the other way."

She changed direction and went the other way.

A few minutes later, Michelle entered the sanctuary wearing a badge.

As she slowly made her way down toward the front, her eyes landed on Bishop Jakes, who was saying, ". . . God didn't fall asleep on the job and the devil came in and wrecked the car. No, God never sleeps and he never slumbers."

The crowd erupted into shouts of "Amen."

"He's in complete control and he knows where you are, and he knows how old you are, and he knows how much time you spent, and he knows what happened to you, and he knows who walked out and left you, and he knows who betrayed you . . ."

Michelle stopped in her tracks.

It was as though Bishop Jakes was talking directly to her. She'd felt that same sensation over the last two nights, but this time Michelle had no doubt this particular message was especially for her.

"He knows who molested you," Bishop Jakes stated. "And he

knows who raped you, and he knows who rejected you, and he knows where you are in life, and he knows about your bills, and he knows about your degrees, and he knows you dropped out of school, and he knows about what you didn't get, and he knows about the health of your child, and he knows about the condition of your neighborhood. Understand that and tell yourself nothing just happens."

Michelle just stood there listening, and realized God was calling out for her.

"Occasionally you can meet somebody and you sense that your destiny is tied to this person. When you spend your life with them, that's all you have. There is no greater bond possible. You'll never be who you were meant to be without them in your life. There is something, there is something about the way they talk, it feeds you."

Bishop Jakes paused for a second, then continued, "It's something about the way they speak that changes you. You didn't meet them by accident. You didn't stumble up and meet them. This didn't just happen. There is a reason that you're in this place. . . ."

Michelle's eyes landed on Todd. She gave him a tiny smile and pointed toward the front.

He nodded.

She resumed her efforts to make it down to the front. Afterward, she would sit with Todd and his family.

Reggie's eyes were locked on the stage where Bishop Jakes was standing. The feelings of panic and fear had passed.

"I'm so sick of talking to people who think that everything just happens. The steps of a good man are ordered by the Lord."

Bishop Jakes pointed toward the audience. "Your steps were ordered. If you hadn't made that mistake you wouldn't even be here right now. God has been behind the curtain like a puppet master pulling strings in your life. It's not that you're smart, it's not that you're great, it's not that you're holy, it's not that you're perfect, it's not that you're good, but God winded you up. He pointed you in the right direction, released you into your destiny, and you are here and you can't get away. . . ."

Reggie nodded, believing that the words Bishop Jakes spoke were meant for him. He didn't want to run anymore. *I'm ready, Lord,* he cried silently. *I don't want the drugs no more . . . I don't wanna chase after other women . . . Cassey . . . she a good woman. . . .*

"Your mistakes were in His will. Your trouble was in His will. Your pain was in His will. I don't care what you went through. . . ."

Reggie's eyes filled with tears as he listened to the sermon. Bishop Jakes had tapped deep down in his soul, bringing to the surface his hurts, his fears and his shame.

The memories he'd repressed for so long were present in his mind. Reggie recalled episode after episode of sexual abuse at the hands of his mother's best friend.

A series of images entered his mind.

One of Michelle as a child. Another of her as a teenager, screaming and cursing at him.

A hot tear rolled down his cheek as the image of her in the strip club came to mind. Reggie would never forget the look of pure hatred he saw in Michelle's eyes the day she stabbed him.

Reliving the pain of what he'd suffered as a child forced him to realize the damage he'd done to her. How different would her life have been if he'd just left her alone, he wondered.

Michelle used to dream of being a singer. Reggie tried to remember the last time he'd heard her sing. It was before the first time he touched her. She never sang another word after that.

Reggie dropped his head in shame. Even when Cassey had questioned him this morning about Michelle, he'd continued to lie. *Lord, I can't tell Cassey that I touched her daughter. I can't tell her that.* As much as he wanted to bare his soul, Reggie just couldn't come clean. *This between you and me, God. I'll go to my grave with this sin.*

"Think about the most damnable thing that ever happened and shout, 'nothing,'" Bishop Jakes instructed his audience.

"Nothing," they proclaimed in unison, including Michelle, who was standing the aisle, too anxious to sit down.

For her, it was the day Reggie stole her virginity. It was the day his terrible act sentenced her to a life of shame. It was a day that forever haunted her dreams. It was the day Michelle learned what it meant to truly hate someone.

"Think about the most embarrassing thing that ever happened in your life and shout, 'nothing.'"

Bishop Jakes's voice was loud over the roar of the audience. "Think about the most impoverished, financially depleting thing that ever happened in your life and shout, 'nothing.'"

Teary-eyed men and women all over the church were standing and waving their hands in the air as they shouted, "Nothing."

"Think about the worst scandal that you ever went through in your life and shout, 'nothing.' Think about people who loved you and walked out and left you and shout, 'nothing.'"

"Nothing," Michelle shouted as she clapped her hands in response to Bishop Jakes's words.

"Think about betrayal on the highest level of your life and shout, 'nothing.' Think about the struggle going on in your job right now and shout, 'nothing.'"

As she listened to Bishop Jakes, Michelle suddenly realized that she was both physically and emotionally exhausted. It was time to allow God to take over in her life. She had come to the conclusion that only God knew a way out of her situation.

All I can be, I haven't become. All I can do, I haven't done. How far I can reach, haven't yet been reached. I am a work that hasn't been completed The words popped into her head without warning. Michelle glanced around as if to see if anyone else had heard them. She searched her memory to find out where she'd heard them spoken.

"If a drug dealer can use chemistry for the streets, he has the potential of becoming a chemist in a pharmaceutical company if his or her life is saved and redirected," the chaplain preached in the prison.

Michelle shook her head in disbelief. He was out of his mind, she thought.

"If a person can prostitute themselves and be a comfort for some stranger, then they have the potential of becoming a psychologist or counselor if they are saved and their lives are redirected."

The prison chaplain met Michelle's hostile gaze and stated, "Everybody has potential. All of you in here can find your way to a street called Straight . . . just pray to Jesus for help. . . ."

His words went in one ear and out the other. Michelle wasn't interested. Being in prison for stabbing Reggie didn't bother her. It was a relief to her to be off the streets and not having to deal with Pervis. In here, she didn't have to face Cassey—hear her painful lament over how she'd lost her mind and how she nearly killed the man that was the only father she'd ever known.

Reggie was a monster, not a father.

Bored, Michelle shifted in her seat, tapping her foot impatiently on the floor.

When the chaplain bowed his head to pray, Michelle stared ahead, her chin tilted up defiantly.

"God, I thank you right now for the way You have come into my life and changed my thoughts and my walk. I praise You, Lord, for taking a sinner like me and allowing me to be used as an instrument in Your kingdom. The road is rough, but the path is clear, God, because it is narrow and I don't have room enough to turn around. I don't want to look back because I might stumble. Thank You, God, for planting my feet on a solid rock and making me into a humble servant."

He paused for a heartbeat before moving on. "I thank You, God, for my ability and my opportunity to evangelize the Good News that Jesus is coming back and we must be ready because You have prepared a place for us. Finally, Lord, I ask that You bless the hearers and the doers of Your Word as Divinely given to me. Amen."

•   •   •

Michelle shook her head. She had been so blind. Those words didn't make sense to her at the time, but she understood now.

Michelle had to make a decision.

Tearfully, she raised her eyes heavenward. "Wash me clean, Heavenly Father," she murmured. "Come into my life and make me whole. . . ."

17

Michelle felt a sudden chill and rubbed her arms to restore the warmth. She glanced around, observing people praying, some praising God and some, like her, crying. She couldn't help but wonder what their lives were like—past and present.

There were people in the sanctuary who were homeless and dirty—yet they were lifting their hands to praise the Lord. Michelle thought about the smelly woman she sat next to on the first night of revival. She'd been repulsed by the woman—but what right did she have? Her, a woman with a dirty past.

There were people in the sanctuary looking to be healed. People who were drug addicts wanting to be freed from their addictions.

Michelle wanted something, too. She wanted to be freed from all the terrible things in her life.

She thought back to the day she walked out of prison.

Oh, how her life had changed in just three days.

Michelle held her purse close to her chest and took a deep calming breath.

The Lord loved her still. . . .

Her eyes watered at that acknowledgment, causing Michelle to blink rapidly.

When she was first told about attending the revival, she wasn't thrilled about it, but Michelle was willing to do whatever it took to get out of prison. She wanted to taste freedom again.

But with the help of Bishop Jakes, she was given a chance to really make something of her life.

Michelle observed him standing on the stage, his arms wide open. He was urging all of them to join him on the street called Straight. He'd asked all of them to bring the things that held them captive—kept them off the path.

She glanced down at her purse and smiled.

Tonight, she would be free of the bonds. Michelle's heart flipped in her excitement. She could feel the beginning of a new life close on the horizon.

Michelle caught Nicole's eye and smiled. She and Bobby looked happy together. It made her feel good seeing her friend with her children. *Nikki's worked so hard for this. She deserves to be happy.*

Seated three rows ahead of her, Twana looked back at her and waved.

Michelle waved back. "Where's Cassey?" she mouthed.

Twana shrugged her shoulders.

Michelle inched closer toward the front. People were everywhere. In the aisles, in the balcony, standing along the sides of the sanctuary.

Michelle continued looking around, scanning row by row searching for Cassey, but couldn't find her anywhere.

Maybe she was in the prayer room.

Michelle glanced over her shoulder, trying to decide if she wanted to attempt to make it back to the prayer room to seek out her mother.

But there was a sea of people behind her and she didn't want to lose her position in the line that was forming. She would see Cassey after the service.

Maybe they would have a chance to talk. Have a real mother-daughter conversation for once in their lives.

Twana didn't miss the way Michelle's eyes kept traveling the sanctuary. She was looking for Cassey.

Michelle loved her mother unconditionally, despite her reluctance to admit it. And Twana had to admit that Cassey loved her daughter. She just didn't know how to show it. If only she'd get rid of Reggie.

Twana shook the thought completely out of her head. Cassey was too needy when it came to men. That's why she allowed Reggie to treat her so badly all these years.

I get lonely, Twana acknowledged. *Real lonely, but I'm not gonna just let any old fool in my life.*

Twana thought about the days when she and Cassey used to run the streets. The things they used to do . . .

A flush crept up Twana's face. *Lord, I'm so sorry. I have no right thinking about stuff like that in here. I'm supposed to be turning my life around. I'm trying, Lord. I'm still a work in progress.*

She stole a peek at Michelle, who was still trying to make it down to the front. *She gon' give her life to the Lord.* The thought made Twana smile. It's what she and Cassey had been praying for.

Where is Cassey? she wondered. *She ain't working tonight.* She leaned forward and searched the rows in front of her as far as she could see them. There was no sign of her friend anywhere.

Twana felt beads of perspiration on her brow and began fanning with her hands. With so many people in the building, it was hot. She prayed someone would think to turn the air up a notch. If not, they ran the risk of someone passing out like last time.

An usher walked over and handed Twana a fan.

"Thank you so much," she uttered in gratitude.

Feeling a little cooler, Twana's gaze traveled to Michelle. Her goddaughter was making her way resolutely toward the altar. Twana was so proud.

The heat was affecting Cassey as well.

She signaled to one of the ushers standing nearby to bring her a fan.

Cassey smiled her thanks and immediately began fanning herself.

Reggie shifted in his seat, bringing her attention to him. She couldn't miss the troubled expression on his face, nor the way his hands shook. He had this faraway look about him and seemed deep in thought.

Her heart went out to him. Cassey hated seeing the man she loved like this. Reggie was clearly in a lot of pain and there was nothing she could do to help him.

She consoled herself with the fact that maybe it had to come to this—maybe Reggie had to reach a roadblock to get him to open his heart to the Lord.

"God, please help him. Help him to find his way to You, dear Lord," she whispered fervently.

Her heart did a little flip because this was what she'd been praying for. Cassey wanted Reggie to be saved. She wanted the same for Michelle.

Cassey glanced over her shoulder to see if she could spot Michelle somewhere in the sanctuary. But there were too many people to see anything, so she gave up.

This was the last night of revival and she prayed it had done her daughter some good.

"... Think about the attitude of your kinfolks and your family members and shout, 'nothing,'" Bishop Jakes roared.

"Nothing," Cassey shouted.

"Think about how your boss is treating you on your job and shout, 'nothing.' Think about that disagreement between you and your children and shout, 'nothing.'"

"Nothing," the audience shouted in unison.

Suddenly and without warning, Reggie put his hands to his face and began sobbing.

Cassey wrapped an arm around him, trying to console him. She could feel his tears wetting her blouse.

"Think about your past life of sin," Bishop Jakes stated. "Your whoremongering, your inappropriateness, your attitude, your dysfunction and shout, 'nothing.' Shout, 'nothing.' Let the devil hear you say 'nothing.' That devil will think he's won if you don't shout 'nothing.'"

"Nothing" could be heard all over the sanctuary.

"The devil will think he's in charge if you don't shout 'nothing.' He'll think he's going to win but you've got to shout 'nothing.'"

Cassey opened her purse and pulled out a tissue, handing it to Reggie.

She pulled out another for her own eyes.

Heal this rift in my family, she prayed silently. *The devil can't win, Dear Lord. He can't have them. . . .*

She jumped up and shouted, "Nothing . . ."

Almost everyone in the church was now on their feet.

Cassey raised her arms to give God praise along with the rest of the congregation.

After a moment, she sank back down in her seat, feeling exhilarated. The spirit of the Lord was in the sanctuary and Cassey could feel it.

She cast a glance Reggie's way. He was still sitting there sobbing like a baby. Embracing him, she murmured over and over again, "It's gon' be all right, honey. Ooh, yes . . . the Lord is faithful . . . He's so good . . . Just give it to Him. Give it all over to Jesus. . . ."

Reggie wept from the pain of his own existence.

He couldn't find words to describe what he was feeling right now, except that he was lost and he desperately wanted to find his way back.

"Give it to Jesus. . . ."

Cassey's words were able to penetrate through the fog in his brain. "I . . . I d-don't . . ." He couldn't finish.

More tears followed.

Reggie felt a certain wretchedness he'd never felt before in his life. He wiped his eyes and tried to stifle his tears. Nearly losing his life the night before had really affected him.

"Open yo' heart to Jesus, honey," Cassey murmured. "Let Him come in, Reggie. Only Jesus can fix all the wrong, but you gotta give Him a chance. Drugs ain't the answer. Sex ain't the answer. . . ."

Reggie knew that what Cassey was saying was right. He needed to turn his life around. Last night when Dupree had that gun to his head, his life passed before his eyes and Reggie didn't like what he saw. He was nothing. Just a man who wasted his life on the wrong things. And although he wasn't ready to die, he felt unworthy of living.

"I want to change, Cassey. I do."

"I know you do, honey. You can't do it by yo'self."

"I don't know how." Reggie held her tight and pleaded with her, "Please help me, Cassey. Please help me."

"I want to." Cassey paused for a minute before continuing. "Reggie, listen to me. You have to give God yo' heart. He is the answer to all yo' problems. As much as I want to take this hurt . . . this pain from you . . . I can't. Only God can help you."

Reggie sat up in his seat.

"I know," he said, barely above a whisper.

"Now listen . . . listen . . . listen closely," Bishop Jakes directed. "I want you to do something. Bring to the altar a tangible

209

symbol of your oppression. It will be your way of saying to God, 'I put this thing before you, Lord, but now I put you first. I want to serve you.'"

Reggie felt inside his jacket. His crack pipe.

His eyes traveled to Cassey.

She was looking down at Bishop Jakes, her eyes wet from unshed tears. Her lips were moving and Reggie knew she was praying for him—for his soul.

Despite all of the things he said and did to her, Cassey loved him and had stayed by his side. Reggie became overwhelmed by the guilt he felt as he saw the damage left from her stroke. He had never considered the idea before, but now it seemed probable. He had most likely been the cause of her having the stroke in the first place.

"This is our final night," Bishop Jakes reminded everyone. "You may not get another chance."

Torn by indecision, Reggie didn't make a move as a steady line began to form and people littered the altar with paraphernalia.

He could feel Cassey watching him—waiting to see if he was going to get up and join the procession to the altar. She would be so disappointed in him if he didn't. Reggie's fingers traveled back to the pipe hidden in his jacket.

The incident of the night before still fresh in his mind, Reggie put both hands to his face.

Bishop Jakes was still urging people to come forward.

Reggie propelled himself to the end of his seat, but his legs didn't feel strong enough to stand. He felt dizzy for a moment, and settled back into his chair.

Out of the corner of his eye, Reggie glimpsed Cassey chewing on her bottom lip and twisting her hands in the fold of her skirt.

He leaned forward to watch the crowd below. People were littering the altar with everything from condoms and pills to sex toys.

Just a few days ago, Reggie might have found this scene hilarious, but not now. It seemed a little pathetic.

"All God's children tryin' to come home," Cassey murmured in a low voice. "That's what you seeing, Reggie."

He could only nod.

"Keep coming," Bishop Jakes encouraged. "Crack pipes, liquor flasks, money, bills, condoms, prescription bottles . . ."

Michelle opened her purse and removed the dress. She held it gently in her arms as she patiently waited her turn.

She was ready to surrender all that had been holding her back. Like Bishop just said—she might not ever get another chance.

Feeling very emotional, Michelle made her way to the altar.

Twana jumped out of her seat and rushed over to embrace her.

"I'm happy for you, Michelle," she whispered. "You doin' the right thing. God is faithful. He'll never let you down."

Through her tears, Michelle nodded and smiled.

She stole a peek over her shoulder to where Todd was sitting.

He winked and gave her an encouraging smile.

She returned her attention to Bishop Jakes. His voice, she decided, had a way of bringing a calm to her troubled soul.

Getting impatient, Michelle pushed her way through the

crowd of people who, like her, wanted to lay down their burdens at the altar.

Michelle wiped at her tears with the back of her hand.

As she walked, she searched through the crowd for Cassey, but Michelle couldn't find her mother anywhere.

Where are you, Mama? I want to share this with you.

18

"Bring down your burdens. Lay them before the Lord. Hand over your addictions, your troubles, your anxiety, your fear," Bishop Jakes continued to urge the congregation.

"Let your old self die before God so that you can be reborn into the family of Christ. Stop running from your past, from your pain, and run into the arms of your Father, Who is waiting to embrace you."

Reggie suddenly shot to his feet, surprising Cassey. He hugged her and whispered, "It's time I gave my life over to the Lord. I can't run no more."

He'd surprised himself by making this decision. Reggie wasn't sure initially that he really wanted to make this type of commitment. He wasn't sure he was ready. But each time he tried to talk himself out of it, the image of Dupree holding the gun to his head popped up in his mind.

Reggie feared that if he didn't give his life over to God, he would die. He was desperately afraid of dying.

"Thank You, Jesus," Cassey hollered. "Thank You, Lord. . . ." Cassey threw her hands up in the air. "Thank You, Lord . . . Thank You. . . ."

Reggie's legs still felt weak and his stomach did somersaults as he made his way down the steps, toward the front.

He wiped away the tears flowing down his face.

It may have been his imagination, but it seemed as if people were stepping to the side as he navigated down to the front.

When he stood before the altar, Reggie reached into his pocket, then hesitated a moment. He wasn't sure about pulling out the crack pipe. With his luck, he'd do it right in front of some policeman.

Then he heard Cassey's voice encouraging him to give all to God.

Reggie eased the crack pipe from the pocket of his jacket and held it in his hands, caressing it. He bent over and laid it on the altar.

For a split second, Reggie had the urge to pick it back up, but someone reached over and shook his hand.

Members of the congregation took turns hugging him and welcoming him into the fold.

Reggie looked over his shoulder at Cassey, who was standing up clapping her hands and smiling. He could see the happiness on her face and he felt good. For once, he'd done something that truly pleased her.

But Reggie knew that he hadn't done this just for Cassey—this was more for him.

He wanted God to save him from himself and from the world.

He fell to his knees and lifted his hands toward heaven.

"Please forgive me, God," Reggie begged.

Someone standing beside him placed a caring arm around him. "Let me pray with you, brother."

"I'm not good enough. . . ."

"Brother, many think they're not good enough or did something so terrible they can't come to God." The man shook his head. "Let me tell you something. This is baloney—just plain flesh thinking. It's wrong thinking, and goes against everything the Bible teaches."

"But I . . ." Reggie couldn't say the words, his deeds too horrible to mention.

"Let God clean up your act. Let the Word and the Holy Spirit do the work. Jesus tells us to ask and it shall be given, and to pray without ceasing. To come unto me. Let me pray with you, brother. Just repeat after me."

The man bowed his head.

Reggie followed suit.

"Lord Jesus Christ, I come to you now, because I am a sinner. Today, Lord Jesus, I repent of my sin, I turn away from my sin, and I turn to You."

Reggie repeated the words.

"I believe, dear Lord, that You died for me. I thank You, Lord, because Your blood covers all my sins. No one else can save me, only Jesus. Right now, I open the door of my heart. Come into my heart, Lord Jesus."

Tears rolled down Reggie's cheeks as he prayed.

"Wash me. Cleanse me, and make me your child. I receive You now by faith. Help me to live for You every day until You come again. I close the door and Jesus is inside. I thank You, Lord Jesus, because today, by faith, I have received You and You have received me. Amen."

"Amen," Reggie repeated.

"Welcome to the family of God, brother." The man reached over and embraced him.

"Thank you," Reggie murmured. "Thank you."

He felt as if a huge weight had been lifted from him.

Twana did a double take.

Surely her eyes were deceiving her. That couldn't be Reggie down there at the altar. She adjusted the floppy hat on her head and leaned forward.

Her eyebrows rose in surprise. It was Reggie.

Twana settled back in her seat. *What in the world is he up to?* she wondered.

Ain't no way he turnin' over a new leaf.

Her gaze shifted to Michelle, who was now just a few yards away from Reggie.

Twana jumped up.

"Excuse me . . . ," she mumbled as she rushed out of the row she was sitting in. She needed to get down to the altar before Michelle saw Reggie. Twana didn't know why, but she had a bad feeling.

People were still trying to make it to the altar.

Twana groaned in frustration. "C'mon, people . . . let me get by. I need to get down there now."

"We all tryin' to get down there. You gonna have to be patient," someone in front of her said.

"You don't understand. . . ."

"Yeah I do. You want to be saved."

"No, I'm trying to save someone. Now pleeze . . . let me through."

Twana made it through only to get caught in another crush of people.

Frantic, she searched around the church, looking for Cassey. If she couldn't get to Michelle, maybe she could reach Cassey.

Twana peered around the line of people, looking for Michelle. She was in front of the altar.

She prayed Michelle didn't see Reggie, and she prayed Reggie didn't see Michelle.

Todd was beside himself with joy when he saw Michelle getting in line. She was giving her life to the Lord.

His Michelle was on her way back to him. He sent up a silent prayer of thanksgiving for her return.

He applauded the courage she possessed and marveled at her strength.

He broke into a big grin when Nicole caught his eye. They were both happy to see Michelle finding her way.

He leaned forward, trying to see what it was that Michelle

was laying on the altar. It looked like a piece of old fabric from what he could tell—he was too far away to be sure.

"What she putting on the altar?" his mother inquired.

"I don't know," Todd responded. "I can't get a good look at it."

"I pray she finds some happiness."

"She will," Todd replied with confidence. "Michelle's gonna be all right after tonight. I can feel it."

Todd struggled to keep his feelings for her under wraps. He didn't want to push so much that it sent Michelle running. He had agreed to give her the space she needed, but Todd was finding it very hard to keep up his end of the deal.

There were a few times when he had to consider that maybe— just maybe—they weren't meant to be together as a couple. Maybe they were just destined to be friends. Good friends.

Todd didn't want to believe that.

His heart belonged to Michelle and always would.

She was here at last.

Michelle breathed a sigh of relief. She held out the tattered dress and let it float from her arms to the floor.

Hands by her sides, she stood there looking up at Bishop Jakes. All around her, people were crying, embracing one another, and praying.

Michelle had one wish. She wished that Cassey were standing before the altar with her. She yearned to feel her mother's arms around her.

She heard someone say, "Praise God, that brother over there just got saved. . . ."

Curious, Michelle turned to her left to see who they were talking about.

Her mouth dropped open in her shock.

Reggie?

Frozen to the spot, Michelle couldn't believe her eyes.

Just a few yards away, he was standing near the altar receiving hugs and congratulations from several members of the congregation.

"If God can save this brother, He can do anything," a man near him stated. "Praise God. . . ."

Saved? Reggie ain't saved.

Her gaze slid over every inch of him, wondering, *How can child molesters go to heaven with their victims? Surely God wouldn't allow such an injustice.*

Bishop Jakes continued calling for lost children to return home. "Bring it . . . bring it . . . marijuana, pornography . . . what are you idolizing? Bring it. . . ."

Putting her hand to her mouth, Michelle swallowed the bile in her throat when she saw Reggie kneel humbly before the altar. He had no place in this building. He was a vile excuse for a human being.

Michelle was so enraged, she was barely conscious of her purse falling to the floor.

She didn't notice that it lay open, revealing the handle of the gun. Her eyes remained on Reggie.

He was her abuser, her sworn enemy, the devil incarnate. . . .

"Nooo. No way." Stunned and confused, Michelle uttered, "This ain't right. I gotta live with him in heaven, too?"

She looked around at the people standing nearby. "How can he go to heaven after all the things he done? It ain't right."

A woman beside her was talking to her, but Michelle shook her head and waved her hand in dismissal. She didn't want to hear it. This was just too much for her to digest right now.

Reggie had a strong sensation that he was being watched.

Fearful that Dupree was somewhere in the sanctuary, Reggie glanced around.

Then he made eye contact with Michelle.

The expression on her face unnerved him. He'd seen that same look of horror on her face before—the day he raped her. Although it never really bothered him before, this time it did.

Reggie looked over his shoulder at Cassey. He was ready to accept blame and make amends, even if it meant losing her. He had to be honest with her and prayed she would one day be able to forgive him. He also had to find a way to help Michelle heal.

He considered his options and decided to approach Michelle first. She'd been the one to suffer the most at his hands.

Reggie rose up, repentant, arms open—wanting to apologize for the way he hurt her. His eyes filled with tears.

He took a step toward her.

"Michelle . . . I'm sorry. I'm so sorry for what I done. Please forgive me. . . ." Reggie wanted to make things right between them, but in order for that to happen, he needed her forgiveness.

Ignoring the curious looks he was receiving from a few of the people standing near them, Reggie continued to approach Michelle.

"I'm so sorry. I was wrong—I know that now and I want . . . Michelle, I need you to forgive me."

19

"What did you think was going to happen, Michelle?"

"I don't know, Bishop. All I remember is just being overcome with fear. It was like I was twelve years old again."

"Do you believe that people can change?"

"Yeah, I do. But do I believe that Reggie changed just by going down to the altar? Overnight?" Michelle shook her head. "No. I don't believe he could've changed just like that.

"I don't know what was going on in his mind that day—I just know when I saw him coming toward me, I freaked out."

Terrified, Michelle glanced around for help.

Memories of Reggie's heinous crimes against her body weighed heavy on her mind. It was at his hand that she'd become the person she was—cold like ice and afraid to love. Because of Reggie, she had lived a life of shame and disappointment with no dreams of anything more.

He advanced on her and Michelle retreated.

"No," she yelled. "Don't touch me."

The gun. The gun was in her purse.

She bent down and reached for the gun, pointing it at Reggie.

"Stay away from me. Don't you ever touch me again," she screamed.

Michelle had no clear thought of where she was anymore—she was completely lost in the past.

"Michelle . . . no . . . please no . . . I'm sorry. . . ." Reggie inched closer. "D-don't do this. . . ."

Crying hysterically, Michelle fired off three shots in rapid succession.

Reggie fell to the floor in a puddle of his own blood.

Screaming, Michelle collapsed, while people were scrambling and trying to get out of harm's way.

20

The gun fell out of Michelle's hand.

In shock, she picked up the dirty, bloodstained dress, and clutched it to her chest as she began to pray.

"Father God. I am so broken, mentally and physically," Michelle cried. "There is no one to comfort me in my pain, Lord. I am nothing but a mockery to everybody. Look where I am now, God. You know all my untold miseries and I come to You for help. . . . Lord, I shot the man who molested me over and over again. Your Word says that You look at the hearts of men. You know my circumstances, Lord, and You know that I am innocent." She held up the dress toward heaven.

"I w-was the v-victim," Michelle bawled as she continued to hold the dress above her head, babbling, "You are a just judge, God . . . I was the victim . . . I-I was the v-victim. . . ."

• • •

One minute they were praising the Lord and then all of a sudden there was a loud noise and pandemonium. It took a moment for Cassey to comprehend all that had taken place.

Stunned, she looked at Reggie lying on the ground, blood everywhere.

He'd been shot.

Cassey's eyes traveled to his shooter.

Michelle.

Her daughter had dropped the gun and picked up what looked like a child's dress. Suddenly she grabbed the gun again and clutched it tight with both hands.

The realization of what had transpired and what Michelle might now do propelled Cassey out of her seat. "Lord, have mercy," she murmured.

She pushed past bodies, familiar and unfamiliar, trying to get down to the front.

Someone grabbed her arm, trying to hold her back.

"Let me go," Cassey yelled. "I got to go to my daughter."

"Let her go," Twana demanded.

Holding out her hand, she said, "C'mon, Cassey. We got to see 'bout Michelle."

Hand in hand, they made their way down to the floor.

When Cassey neared Reggie's body, she stopped in her tracks.

Twana grabbed her by the arms and stated, "Michelle needs you, Cassey. There's nothing you can do for Reggie, but your daughter is over there scared to death and may hurt herself. Do you want to lose both of them tonight?"

"He's breathing, Twana." Cassey released a sigh of relief.

"Reggie's not dead. I got to go over there and let him know I'm here."

"You can't do this to Michelle. Not now when it's obvious she needs you so much."

Tears rolling down her face, Cassey pulled her hand from Twana's. "I got to let him see me."

"Your daughter needs you," Twana kept insisting. "Can't you see this is what it's all about? Michelle is hurting, Cassey. She's scared, even though she won't admit it. How can you abandon her now?"

Twana pointed to Michelle. "Look at her. Look at your daughter."

Cassey turned to watch Michelle. She was kneeling in front of the altar, the gun still in her hands but now resting in her lap, her head bent in resignation.

Praying for what? Cassey wondered. *Forgiveness?*

She turned back to where Reggie lay bleeding. His chest was still rising and falling. "Lord, please don't let him die," she prayed.

It took Cassey a moment to realize that it was Bishop Jakes who was kneeling beside Reggie, holding his hand and praying for him. She suddenly burst into another round of tears. "Oooh Lord, what'll I d-do? I d-don't know w-what to d-do."

Twana sent Cassey a disgusted look before walking off. She crossed the room in quick strides to reach Michelle.

Cassey took two steps toward her daughter, but then paused when she heard her name called.

She turned and looked.

Reggie's eyes were open and on her. His lips were moving.

"Sister Jordan," the man bent over Reggie called out. "He wants to see you."

He needed her.

Wiping her eyes, Cassey rushed over to his side.

She pulled out a tissue and tried to wipe his face. "I'm here, honey."

His mouth was still moving as if he were trying to tell her something.

Cassey leaned down close to his lips to hear.

Reggie's voice was a harsh whisper. "I . . . I . . . I'm sorry. . . ."

"Honey, you don't have nothing to be sorry 'bout. You gave your life to the Lord. All yo' sins been washed away. Now I don't want you worryin' no more. I want you to save yo' strength so you can get better." Cassey's voice broke. "I-I w-want you to come h-home, Reggie."

He tried to speak.

"It's gon' be all right. Just lay here. The paramedics should be here soon."

Cassey glanced over at Bishop Jakes. "Someone called them, didn't they?"

"They should be here shortly," he confirmed.

Suddenly Reggie started to convulse. Blood dribbled out of his mouth and down his chin.

"Don't you dare leave me," Cassey cried. "Reggie, you can fight this."

His breathing was slowing down, she could see it.

In the distance, Cassey heard the sirens. "Can you hear that? That's the paramedics. They'll be here real soon.

"C'mon, Reggie," she whispered. "Hold on. Help is on the way. Just hold on."

. . .

Twana approached Michelle carefully and knelt down beside her.

"Honey, it's gon' be all right. . . . Just put the gun down. You're safe . . . you safe now, Michelle."

"I'm the victim," she cried. "He can't g-go to h-heaven with - m-me."

Kissing her cheek, Twana whispered, "It's okay, baby. It's gon' be all right."

"I just wanted to be washed clean," Michelle whispered "I didn't want h-him to touch me. I had to keep him from touching me with his filthy hands. I wanted to be clean."

Twana stroked Michelle's cheek the way she used to when she was a little girl. "I know, baby. I know what that feels like."

"I just wanted to be clean, and now I don't deserve anything," Michelle whimpered.

"Michelle, put that gun down and look at me," Twana ordered. She did as she was told.

"You're safe now. Do you understand what I'm saying to you?" Michelle nodded. "Is he dead?"

Twana glanced over to where Reggie lay. "I don't know, baby girl. If he's not . . ." She sighed. "I don't think he's gon' make it, Michelle."

"I killed him."

"The police have been called," Twana announced. "When they get here—"

"I'm going back to prison," Michelle finished for her. "It's where I belong."

"Ooh, baby girl. . . ."

Michelle stiffened. "Cassey?" she managed through tight lips.

"Honey . . . ," Twana began.

Shaking her head, Michelle held up her hand to silence her.

They heard a commotion behind them and Twana knew the police and the paramedics had arrived.

"Michelle, they're here."

They were suddenly surrounded by policemen with guns drawn.

"The gun's right there," Twana shouted. "She not gon' hurt nobody."

Closing her eyes, she prayed, "Lord, help Michelle. . . ."

He could hear people screaming, talking, and moving all around him. Cassey was still sitting there beside him, holding his hand.

Reggie tried to speak to her, but no words would come.

Michelle had shot him.

He had been fortunate to survive the time she stabbed him, but this time he feared that she might have succeeded in killing him.

It happened so fast, he thought. *I never saw it coming. I had my faults just like the next man. But I was working on them. I just thought I had more time. There was so much I wish I could've said to Michelle . . . to Cassey . . . to God . . . but I just ran out of time. . . ."*

The room dimmed in his view, his surroundings grew darker and darker.

His breathing became labored and it was soon hard to focus.

A shadow loomed before him.

Reggie blinked for a clearer view.

It was Bishop Jakes. His lips were moving, but Reggie couldn't hear the words. He assumed he was praying for his soul.

Reggie could feel his life ebbing away.

He summoned what little strength he had left to look toward the heavens.

God, I just needed a little more time. . . .

Reggie was dead.

Cassey felt numbness spread through her body when she received the news. She'd pretty much known that he wasn't going to make it.

He was gone—killed by her daughter.

Cassey closed her eyes, unable to cope with the realization that Michelle had murdered Reggie in cold blood.

How could things have gone so horribly wrong?

Earlier tonight, Cassey had been rejoicing over the fact that Reggie had given his life to the Lord. Now he was gone.

"This is not what I prayed for," she muttered softly. "I wanted us to be a family."

Someone embraced her.

Cassey was unresponsive. She didn't want to feel anything ever again. She didn't want to talk, cry—anything. She just wanted to turn the clock back.

Why, Michelle? Why did you have to kill him?

Cassey's eyes traveled to the tattered dress lying near the altar. Her heart was heavy.

She refused to consider what it meant to Michelle, or what it meant to Reggie. He was gone and Cassey saw no need to rehash all the pain and heartache.

She couldn't deny that she felt a spark of anger toward her daughter. Michelle had humiliated them all with this tragedy. She'd murdered the man Cassey loved. Yeah, she was very angry.

Twana would blame her, of course, and she would lecture Cassey on being a good mother. She might even say that Reggie deserved to die.

Cassey had to admit she was being a bit unfair. Twana would never go that far. She couldn't stand him, but she would never wish him dead.

The police had Michelle handcuffed and were reading her her rights.

She couldn't summon up the strength to go over and check on Michelle herself. Cassey wasn't sure she could have a conversation with her daughter right now. She was afraid of saying something she could never take back.

They had already lived their lives with too much regret.

Todd was heartbroken.

She was so close, Lord. So close.

"I told you that girl is troubled," his mother whispered. "Something ain't right in her head."

"She was scared, Mom. Didn't you see the look on her face? She thought Reggie was gonna hurt her. I think she was having a flashback or something. But whatever it was, Michelle got scared and she freaked out."

Todd blinked back his tears. "I wanted to protect her. Why wouldn't she let me help her? I knew something wasn't right in that house. I knew it."

"Honey, you did all you could for her," his mother assured him. "She's in God's hands now."

"There must be something I can do. Got to be."

"You can pray for her," his mother suggested. "We'll all pray for her." She held out her hand to him. "Ain't no time like the present. . . ."

Taking her hand, Todd closed his eyes and began to say a prayer. "Our Father in Heaven, I'm coming to You on behalf of Michelle, a young woman caught up in this snare of the devil. Inadvertently, she has taken a wrong step somewhere and is now in a situation that she cannot come out of by herself. Almighty Father, I come to You because Your Word says that You will spare the poor and needy, and save the souls of the needy. You are a gracious, heavenly Father and so full of compassion, slow to anger and great in mercy. You are good to all. Oh Lord, I ask that You save Michelle by Your righteous right hand. Allow her to take refuge in the shadow of Your wings. Become her shelter and a strong tower from the enemy. In Jesus' name I pray. Amen."

"Amen," his mother and several people around him uttered in unison.

Todd opened his eyes and found several prayer circles formed around the sanctuary. He didn't know if they were praying for Michelle or Reggie or both.

"Mom, I need you to do me a big favor. Take Mia home and put her to bed. I'm going to the police station."

She shook her head in disapproval. "Todd, I don't th—"

He cut her off. "I want her to know she's not alone."

"Okay."

He kissed her on the cheek. "Thanks, Mom. I'll see you later."

"Be careful, Todd."

"She's not gonna hurt me."

Todd made his way to the nearest exit.

I'm coming, Michelle. You won't have to go through this alone.

Sobbing, Michelle half listened as one of the detectives read her rights. She had heard it all before.

She focused her attention on Cassey, who was crying as if she'd lost her best friend.

Michelle was filled with profound sadness. She would soon be on her way back to prison. Her mother had rejected her yet again and this time it was more than her heart could take.

When Cassey looked up at her, Michelle dropped her eyes, wanting to avoid the look of disgust she knew she would find there.

Out of the corner of her eye, Michelle caught sight of Nicole. She was crying and Bobby was consoling her.

She knew Nicole would be blaming herself and Michelle wanted to reassure her that it wasn't her fault. Maybe she would write her a letter.

Her arms hurt from the position in which the police had her handcuffed, but she wasn't going to complain.

She dropped her head as they led her past the yellow tape, curious onlookers, and scared church members.

She heard Todd calling her name, but she wouldn't look up. Michelle couldn't face him right now. He'd had such high hopes for them and now . . .

Her biggest regret was that his daughter had to witness the execution of a man that wasn't worthy to grace the inside of any church.

Michelle's eyes filled with tears. She blinked rapidly to keep them from falling.

I was so close, she thought as she was led out of the sanctuary.

Outside, she barely noticed the paramedics carrying Reggie on a gurney and putting it into the ambulance. The police led her to a waiting patrol car and placed her inside.

Michelle caught a glimpse of Cassey before she was driven away.

"Mama," she whispered. "What do you have to say now? Do you even care that I'm on my way back to prison?"

The week after Cassey buried Reggie, she went to see Michelle.

They sat facing one another in uncomfortable silence.

"I . . . I . . . wasn't the best mother to you, but I did my best."

Michelle nodded.

"I used to think about us," Cassey began. "I used to dream that one day we'd get past all the anger. I wanted us to be able to talk to one another."

Michelle didn't respond.

"We all make mistakes, Michelle. I made plenty of them." Cassey wiped at her eyes. "This is not how I wanted yo' life to turn out. That's why I wanted Bishop Jakes to see if he could help you in some way. I'd seen so many people saved during our revivals . . . I wanted that for you, Michelle. I wanted you to have a second chance. I wanted yo' life to change."

"Mission accomplished," Michelle blurted out. "It's sure changed."

"This is not what I meant. I don't want to have to see you behind bars."

"Cassey, this is my life. This is what my life became the day Reggie laid his hands on me."

"I thought revival could help. . . ."

Michelle stood up suddenly. "Cassey, go home."

"But . . ."

"I can't do this. I can't see you like this. Please leave and don't come back, Cassey."

Michelle signaled for the guard to take her away.

Once she was back in the safety of her cell, Michelle released the tears she'd been holding back. It broke her heart to see how much Cassey appeared to have aged just in a matter of a few days.

Michelle supposed her mother was grieving the loss of Reggie and her daughter.

When Reggie died, Michelle thought she'd feel some sort of elation. A certain peace that came with the fact that she was finally free of him.

But that feeling never came.

Her heart was heavy that she'd taken the life of another human being. It didn't make her feel better knowing that it was someone her mother loved.

Michelle had shot him to protect herself, but she wasn't prepared for the torment that followed.

That night she fell to her knees praying to God, begging for
His forgiveness.

21

"Once I was trying to help a little squirrel that had accidentally slipped into the house through an open door," Michelle began. "You see, Bishop, when I was a little girl I used to love watching those squirrels from my bedroom window—watching them dart in and out of hiding. They looked so cute and playful. . . ."

She raised her eyes to meet his. "Well, there's nothing cute and playful about a squirrel trapped in the corner of your kitchen. He ran frantically in circles and bared his teeth at me. Here I was—wanting to help him, and this little squirrel kept runnin' 'round wild. I kept getting closer until he bit me.

"I still have the scar." Michelle showed him a tiny mark on her hand.

"Since I been in here, I been thinking about that little squirrel. I finally realized that I was moving in too close and it scared him.

If I'd backed away a bit, he woulda been able to get his whits about him and figure out how to get out of the house. I knew I wasn't gonna hurt him, but the squirrel didn't know it."

Michelle picked up the little house she'd built during their conversation and examined it.

"I didn't understand how God could forgive a man like that," Michelle stated. "I didn't understand why I should have forgiven him. I struck out and fought back because I felt cornered. Now I do understand. You can never really get even."

"Michelle, do you believe that what you did was the right thing to do?"

She shook her head. "No, I don't, Bishop. What I did was wrong. No matter what he did to me, it was wrong. When you talk to God again, ask Him if He'll forgive me . . . I know I can't bring a life back. . . ."

Michelle paused a moment, summoning the courage to say, "Could you do something else for me? Tell my mother that I love her. Tell her I've always loved her. Ask her if we can get to know each other. No matter what I felt about her, I didn't have a right to take something from her. . . ."

"I will," he promised.

Bishop Jakes rose to his feet, saying, "Well, I want you to know that I've been praying for a little girl. Praying that she wasn't dead. That she would make it through this. I just needed to make sure. I know now that she's alive and well. I know that even though she's bound by these bars, her heart is no longer held captive by her past, her demons. You continue to stay free, you hear me?"

Michelle gave him a genuine smile and nodded. "Good-bye, Bishop."

"Good-bye, Michelle."

She summoned the guard to let Bishop Jakes out of the cell.

Before he walked away, Bishop Jakes stood in the doorway, one foot in the cell and the other in the corridor—the path to freedom.

They shared a smile and then he left.

Michelle jumped up, her matchstick house forgotten for the time being, and peered through the bars until she couldn't see him anymore.

Closing her eyes, Michelle began to sing.

As Bishop Jakes made his way back down the corridor, he heard a voice, singing, ". . . rise, Sally, rise . . . Wipe your weeping eyes . . . Put your hands on your hips and let your backbone slip . . ."

He paused for a moment, listening to Michelle.

"Awww . . . shake it to the east . . . awww . . . shake it to the west . . . awww, shake it to the very one that you love the best."

Bishop Jakes silently gave thanks to God.

Michelle was alive and well. He was confident that she would survive her incarceration just as she'd survived all that happened to her. Michelle's will to live was strong.

EPILOGUE

Six months after her visit with Bishop Jakes, Michelle Jordan's death sentence was overturned. At her new trial, the original murder conviction was reduced to manslaughter.

Now, two years later, Michelle was being released on parole. She was going to be walking out of prison for the last time.

Her life had changed.

Since that first visit, Bishop Jakes came to see her often. He prayed with her, prayed for her, and helped her develop a personal relationship with God. He encouraged her and gave her hope that she really could turn her life around. He'd even suggested that she give her testimony to other women who had been abused.

Initially, she wondered what advice she could possibly give them, but then as time moved forward, Michelle realized that all she had to do was speak the truth.

She'd been born into a family with a generational curse of abuse. She'd been victimized most of her life, and for a time, she'd chosen to be a victim. But through God's loving mercy and His grace, Michelle discovered that her life could become a testament to God's faithfulness. No matter how she chose to live her life, God had the final say.

She would be going to the cathedral this coming Sunday—she had much to be thankful for. And after the service she would be meeting with Bishop Jakes. There were some women he wanted her to meet in connection to a battered women's shelter.

The idea of sharing her story with other woman who found themselves in similar situations appealed to Michelle. She'd had to learn the hard way, but hoped through her experiences others would choose the right path and not follow her example.

She'd heard someone say once that you had to go through some things in order to have a testimony. Michelle knew her life was a testimony—there was no doubt about it.

Todd was another person who had stayed in her corner throughout the entire ordeal, despite her many attempts to force him out of her life. He had written to her regularly and visited whenever he could. He'd promised Michelle that he would always be there for her and she believed him. Todd was a loyal friend.

Michelle hadn't heard much from Nicole, outside of an occasional postcard here and there. Todd had told her that Nicole was seeing her children on the weekends. Michelle was pleased by the news and hoped her friend was faring well.

Michelle walked out of the prison and was startled by the brightness of the sun. Using a hand to shade her eyes, Michelle looked around for Twana.

She dropped her hand at the sight of a lone woman standing outside a car, glancing nervously about.

Michelle did a double take, not believing her eyes.

She stood in one spot, afraid to breathe or even move for fear the vision would evaporate.

She took a tentative step, then another; the whole while she kept watching the woman as she walked.

Twana jumped out of the car, saying, "She begged me to let her come. I hope you don't mind."

Walking up to her mother, she said, "Hi, Cassey."

"You okay?"

Michelle nodded. "Yeah. How 'bout you?"

"I'm fine. I'm glad you're out." Cassey walked around the car to the passenger side. "Let's go home."

Twana touched Michelle on the arms and asked, "You ready?"

Grinning, Michelle nodded. "Yeah, I'm ready. I'm finally ready to go home."